A SELKIE'S SECRET

A FOLK HAVEN NOVELLA

LAUREN CONNOLLY

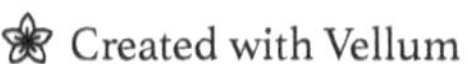 Created with Vellum

ACKNOWLEDGMENTS

Thank you to my parents for showing me so many lovely Georgia lakes. Thank you to my helpful beta readers Rosalind, Marty, Rebekah, and Kimberly. And of course, thank you to my editor Jovana, who has once again cleaned up all the messy sentences I made. You all are amazing!

CONTENT WARNING

*This book includes scenes involving a near-death accident, a DUI
incident, and mutilation in relation to controlling magic.*

1

ISLA

As a responsible thirty-year-old woman, I have accepted that I finally need to collect my fated mate.

Hopefully, he will make the task easy.

I approach the front door of the MacNamara homestead. The collection of houses this selkie clan has on this expanse of lakefront property might be enough to earn the label of *compound*. But that word is too clinical for this family. And *estate* is too grand.

The moment I push through the door, a familiar face greets me.

"Isla! You came." Sorcha MacNamara, matriarch of the family and host of today's backyard barbecue, bustles down the front hall to stop in front of me, a sunburn flush on her normally pale white cheeks.

She reaches out to give my shoulder a squeeze, and I appreciate her remembering my preference. The woman is a hugger. She pulls people in tight to her breast, wrapping them in strong, loving arms, and even goes so far as to wiggle them

I

around while the embrace happens, as if needing to shake her love into them.

The first time I watched the spectacle, all I could do was stare in horror.

Then, she turned to me.

But even at the age of four, I knew what I wanted—as well as what I did not.

When she leaned in, I held up staying hands and expressed a firm, "No, thank you."

Unlike many adults, Mrs. MacNamara listened. When she asked how she could greet me, I provided the shoulder option, and she has kept to it ever since. Even when it's been years since I last saw her.

"I thought it was time I came," I offer.

The woman's smile stays soft on her pretty, round face. "Well, come on in, girl. Everyone is in the kitchen or out back. The kids are about to take pictures in their fancy clothes."

Tonight is Folk Haven High School's prom, and since the MacNamara parents love to host a gathering, they've decided to throw the town's biggest pre-prom party. Which will no doubt bleed into a during-prom celebration. As well as a post-prom shindig.

All the MacNamara children graduated high school a decade or more ago, but that has never stopped their parents from celebrating. Everyone knows the school event is an excuse to invite half the lake over.

The thought of so many people crammed into this place has my skin tightening.

"Is Owen here?"

Sorcha throws me a curious look over her shoulder as we traverse her large yet comfortable house, dodging chatting partygoers along the way. "He is. Seems like most of the town is. And some guests"—she lowers her voice—"are humans. So, keep that in mind when conversing."

"Of course." Keeping the fact that I'm a mythical creature a secret is normal for me.

I spent years living in Portland, Oregon and no one in that city had reason to believe a selkie was walking among them. Even in Folk Haven, a town with a larger mythic population percentage than anywhere else in the world, a good portion of people I interact with on a daily basis are humans.

I know how to be circumspect.

Unfortunately, this means I'll have a harder time managing a candid conversation about matehood. Surely, I can convince Owen to join me in a quiet room somewhere.

We arrive in a kitchen filled with warmth and laughter and people. Lots of people. I clutch my bag closer to my side to avoid inadvertent touching.

"Look who I found at the front door," Mrs. MacNamara announces to the group, like I'm an exciting addition to the party.

I'm not.

My appeal is in my unlikeliness to spill or break something in another person's home. Not to provide entertainment in any way—unless this group would like to start a debate team–like discussion centering around electrical engineering, I'm not on the top of anyone's social list.

Still, I do my best to smile at the assembly and acknowledge the waves in my direction. I know many of these people from my early years spent in Folk Haven. They know exactly how much to expect from me.

"Hi, Isla," a husky voice calls my attention, and I find Moira MacNamara—the eldest of the MacNamara siblings—approaching. "Are you here for fun or to warn us that the dam is about to break and flood our party?"

I cross my arms over my chest, clasping my elbows to make myself more compact as teenagers in formalwear scoot past me in the crowded area. "You would receive notice of that through emergency alerts. And if the dam were to fail, Lake Galen's water level would slowly lower. Only those downstream would need to worry about flooding hazards."

Moira stares at me, her smile staying in place. Waiting.

"You were joking." *I should have realized.*

"And I always enjoy your practical response more than half-hearted laughter." She leans in to mime an air kiss an inch away from my skin. Another agreed-upon greeting. "Glad to see you out of your office." She turns toward the other side of the room. "Calder," Moira yells her brother's name. "Get Isla a ginger beer, one shot of vodka, and three lime wedges."

The youngest MacNamara grins over at me from his spot at the bar and gives a wave of acknowledgment. I nod back, a content hum filling my body that this family knows me so well. Growing up, I always felt more comfortable in their household than my own, where the rules were looser and love flowed without the undercurrent of anxiety. Hopefully, this familiarity will help me meld into the MacNamara clan once I officially mate their brother Owen.

If only I could find him in the crowd.

Moira gets caught up in another conversation while I move to collect my drink from Calder.

"Hey, Isla. Done earning your PhD?" he asks while staring over my shoulder.

I nod. "Six months ago." Which is why I returned to Lake Galen. My educational and professional goals have been reached—for now. Time to pursue personal matters.

"That's impressive." He lowers his voice. "I'm actually working on my master's in business. Tougher than I thought, going back to school."

"It's a good choice. You'll likely earn a high GPA and find the degree beneficial."

Calder's cheeks color—a habit I remember him having whenever people discuss him in a positive manner.

"That's nice of you to say."

I shrug. "It's the truth."

Most people who return to earn a degree later in life take their studies more seriously and earn higher grades. They also tend to choose degrees that more closely align with their careers, meaning the education will be more useful.

But I'm sure he knows that.

"Hey, uh, did you happen to see anyone else out front when you first got here?"

"Please be more specific." I sip my drink and mentally list off the people I observed when walking from my car to the house.

"She ... well ... she's this beautiful woman. Dark hair like yours but a lot longer." He eyes my inch-long tresses before glancing back at the door. "Sometimes, she wears glasses. Her name is Delta. New to town."

"I didn't see anyone like that."

The man stares at the cups he's been stacking in an impractical pyramid formation. "Oh."

"If I meet a dark-haired woman named Delta, I'll inform her that you're looking for her."

Calder gives me a full-faced smile. "Thanks for looking out."

After a nod, I ease away, noticing how a larger crowd has formed around the bar, which means around me. A greater population of people does increase the likelihood of locating Owen, but the presence of so many bodies presses against my skin in an uncomfortable way. I head for the back door, discovering another MacNamara sibling sitting by himself on the porch. But it's the wrong one—again.

"Hello, Seamus."

The man turns to me, brushing curly brown hair out of his eyes. Moira and Calder have the same unruly mass as their brother, but Owen shaved all his off at the start of our senior year in high school and never stopped, last I checked. A practical choice.

"Isla. Good to see you." Seamus's smile is reserved in the same way I imagine mine often is.

However, I've watched this man become boisterous and outspoken when among his family. I'm never boisterous and only occasionally outspoken. Normally, the anomaly occurs at work when a man attempts to tell me how to do a job I was hired for.

"You're not enjoying the party," I point out.

His smile widens, and I wonder why the fates did not pair the two of us together. Our personalities are a much closer match.

But maybe the gods prefer variety in their pairings.

"Are you?" Seamus watches me as I sip the drink his younger brother made me.

"This tastes good, and I have a task to complete. I enjoy striving for and reaching goals."

"And drinking vodka while doing it?"

"That helps." We share a smile. "Where is Owen?"

Seamus raises his eyebrows until they disappear behind the curls that still linger over his forehead. "Down at the dock. You need him?"

"Possibly." I stroll away, heading for the stone path that leads down to the large dock, which juts proudly out into the greenish-blue waters of Lake Galen.

Do I need a mate?

Not particularly.

Do I want one?

I'm here, so it would seem that, on some level, I do.

In that case, yes, I do need Owen.

After skillfully maneuvering through another crowd by the water that must surpass triple digits, I finally spot him. Owen MacNamara stands on the far edge of the dock. As I watch, he tilts his head back, downing a beer in a few deep swallows, his strong neck muscles working with each pull. Everything about Owen is strong. The man has a broad chest and defined arms, all on display, as he's currently shirtless. In the years I've spent away, he's gained more mass to his figure. Not that I'm complaining. There are many ways that ample muscle is useful, both inside and outside of intimate relations.

He is a view to be admired, and I appreciate his form as I approach.

"Hello, Owen."

At the sound of his name, the man faces me, a smile lighting up his broad features.

Promising.

"Isla! It's been forever."

An exaggeration, but I'll allow it as he reaches forward to squeeze my shoulder in much the same way his mother did. Soon, we'll have to elevate our forms of intimacy, but for now, I am content with the affectionate greeting.

That contentment evaporates when Owen steps back and hooks an arm around the waist of a tall woman. Her hair holds a curl much tighter than his, and her skin is darker than his pale Celtic ancestry could ever hope to achieve.

I would know, having descended from the same area of the world as him.

"Ramona, this is Isla. An old friend. Isla, this is Ramona. She's a professor in the Environmental Studies Department at Ramla University."

My conclusions deviate. One part of my brain informs me I should feel some sort of jealousy. My future mate has partnered with an attractive, intelligent woman who is prime competition for his affections.

Yet another section of my brain points out how perfectly her professional interests align with Owen's, as he runs his own recycling company that serves all of Lake Galen and the nearby town of Folk Haven. Perfect pairings always bring a sense of ease to my nerves when they are on edge. And nothing puts me more on edge than a crowded party.

My attention longs to focus on the lake surrounding the dock. Not many people are swimming. Despite the warmth of the day, Lake Galen holds onto a chill through the spring. But the cold temperature would never bother a selkie. Approximately thirty feet out, the water is empty. Under the surface, just there, I could find a section of peace. Quiet solitude.

But I can't leave. Not when I have a mate to procure.

"I enjoy meeting people in the field of academia. They tend to speak of their area of study with great passion and in-depth knowledge." I hold out my hand for her to shake.

Ramona smiles wide at me. "Most times, people can't get me to shut up about it. Luckily, Owen is a fan."

"Because of his company." I nod in understanding and try not to sigh.

Owen watches his date with the fascination of the newly infatuated. The sight doesn't spark the mixture of anger and doubt I associate with jealousy.

Instead, I feel as if I ran a long race, only to come upon another hill. One more grueling leg before I can rest. One last obstacle to overcome before I can settle in with the man the fates have chosen for me.

Best I push on. Try to establish my claim. We've never had a frank conversation about our fated-mate status. I am aware there are certain selkies who, while they still pray to The Finned One along with the other gods, don't believe the lore we followed in the past still applies. If the MacNamara family falls in this group, then I will need to convince Owen that I am his perfect match by other means. If only I were charming, I could attempt to dazzle him with my wit. Or if I were funny, I might try a joke.

Why can't I woo a selkie mate by presenting him a well-

formatted résumé? My academic and professional accolades are numerous and impressive when typed in a bulleted list.

As I consider my mate-catching avenues, I notice movement over Owen's shoulder.

Then, *he* steps forward, and I grind my teeth against a groan.

Finn Hammond.

The man is dark-haired and beautiful, like the woman Calder searches for.

And he's staring at me. A bad habit Finn formed in high school.

The problem with his attention has never been that the pressure of his gaze is unwelcome. It's more that I find myself making unconscious adjustments for it.

When his gray-blue eyes rest on me, I turn, so the side of my face with more pleasing angles faces him.

My voice increases volume, as if intent on including him in the conversation.

My fingers flex with the need to set his messy black hair to rights.

My teeth bite into my lower lip to keep my mouth from ...

Doing something.

"Hi, Isla." The way he says my name is entirely inappropriate.

Only I've yet to identify the reason why that is.

"Finn Hammond. It's been three years since I last saw you."

And I remember the day, the hour, the minute exactly, but I realize just in time that those are not details people tend to share with one another.

He steps closer, tilting his chin down to hold my gaze, encouraging me to stare back at him. "It's been two years since I saw you."

"I—no. What?" Only Finn does this. Makes me trip across my words as if his statements were sticks on a normally smooth-paved path. "How is it you've seen me more recently than I saw you?"

The man has the gall to shrug. "Maybe you weren't paying attention."

"Incorrect. I always pay attention."

One of his thick, dark brows rises. "Do you?" he asks, as if I'd lie about this.

"Of course. When I last saw you was at Coffee & Claws. It was raining, but you had forgotten your rain jacket, so your red shirt was wet." The material clung to his chest in a distracting way. I almost suggested he remove it. "You ordered a hot choco-late. And that was three years ago. See? I pay attention."

As Finn continues to study me, I wait for him to admit that he was wrong.

"Where's Owen?"

"*Where's Owen?*" I repeat the odd question once and then twice in my head before I comprehend the arrangement of the words. When the meaning clarifies, I jerk my head around and realize that in the short moments of speaking to Finn, Owen and his date wandered off.

And I didn't realize it because I wasn't paying attention.

Damn it.

I turn back to Finn to find him still intently watching me, absentmindedly tracing his thumb over a thin scar on his fore-arm. There was a time when we were teenagers, I considered if Finn's staring might have been caused by romantic interest.

What a disaster that would have been.

If attempting to establish a relationship with Owen—a man of my own kind—is a jog up a steep hill, then dating Finn would be akin to scaling a mountain.

The man is human after all.

That fact alone would cause my parents to expire on the spot. Another selkie or nothing. No doubt they'd rather I live a life of spinsterhood, wrapped in bubble wrap and stored in a bulletproof box in their attic.

A romantic relationship with Finn is impossible.

Why am I even pondering the impossibility? Owen is my mate.

Or he will be soon enough.

"You don't need to stare at me so hard," I inform him. "You'll give yourself a headache."

Finn blinks, his head giving a slight jerk, as if he didn't realize what he was doing.

Maybe he didn't. Sometimes, when I'm pondering a particularly challenging problem at work, I will retreat fully into my brain, only to come back to myself and realize I've been gazing at a wall. Or a lamp. Or a trash can.

I hope my colleagues don't assume I am fascinated by trash receptacles.

Am I a trash can to Finn?

The thought encourages me to retreat into myself even more than Owen's quick abandonment did. Which is unacceptable because I am required to care much more about Owen's opinion than any others.

Starting today.

Long ago, the gods made it clear that Owen MacNamara was my fated mate. Not Finn Hammond.

The human is not mine and never will be.

2

———

FINN

She's back.

Thank God. Or thank the gods, as her kind like to say.

The sight of Isla Brown still has me entranced even though I've had all my life to get over my infatuation. I've known since I was sixteen that nothing can ever happen between Isla and me.

Not after one shitshow of a night.

"I can't be expected to pay attention when someone is actively distracting me." Isla turns warm brown eyes on me after realizing Owen disappeared.

People might scoff, hearing me describe anything about Isla as warm. With her blunt way of speaking, most everyone considers her to be robotic. Cold.

But she's just honest.

And that honesty heats me up. Like everything else about her.

"Is that what I was doing?"

Vague questions always catch her attention. She wants to

sand off their uneven corners. Organize them with clear-cut answers.

"Yes. Although I doubt it was intentional."

But it was. Isla's focus often lands on Owen, and I have an idea why. He saved her life. Perfectly normal for Isla to develop hero worship for the guy. Maybe I should stop trying to distract her when Owen is around. But I can't help the painful tug of jealousy in my chest whenever Isla stares at my friend, her focus trained solely on him.

"Your hair is shorter than the last time I saw you. Two years ago," I repeat the time frame. Giving her another rough edge to catch on.

Isla bites into her plump lower lip as her eyes spark, every ounce of her attention adhering to me. Her hand curls in an unrelenting grip around the strap of the bag hanging from her shoulder. She wants to tell me I'm wrong. But both things I said are accurate. Her ebony hair sits in a pixie cut that shows off all the curves and angles of her face.

Which isn't how it looked two years ago.

"Fine," she relents. "When did you see me that I didn't see you?"

I consider teasing her more, but then I'd risk her getting frustrated and leaving. Isla doesn't stay in conversations she doesn't want to.

"I visited a friend in Portland two years ago. We were leaving a brewery, and I saw you walking on the other side of the street."

Isla's brow furrows, creating a V-shaped wrinkle above her nose that I want to trace. "Why didn't you say hello to me?"

Why?

The truth is, I was too stunned. Which I shouldn't have been.

When I'd booked my flight to Portland, I had known that Isla was in the same city, studying at a university there and writing up her dissertation. I'd thought about trying to get her phone number. Asking her to meet up.

But I'd denied myself. Something that's much easier to do when the temptress is not standing directly in front of me, wearing a sundress. She had on a dress that day too. A long green one that swirled around her legs as she walked purposefully down the sidewalk.

And by the time I recovered from the random sighting, Isla had already turned a corner.

I couldn't let her go. I chased after her, sprinting across the street, dodging cars and pedestrians as my friend shouted behind me. As I turned the same corner, I saw the skirt of her dress disappear into the backseat of a car. Before I could reach the spot, the car pulled away.

Taking her out of my life again.

"What would you have done if I had?"

Her brows dip further. "Said hello back."

Of course. So simple. Why do her candid statements wreck me? All I can think about is pulling her into my arms and kissing her neck while she tries answering my questions with the same neutral tone. Until she can't keep steady because of her gasping.

"Next time, say hello," Isla instructs me before turning her back. Leaving me.

I should let her go. That's what I tell myself every time.

And every time, I fail to heed the warning.

"How does the dam work?"

Isla pauses mid-step and then slowly rotates to face me, eyes wide. "What do you want to know?"

I've got her back. "Everything. I didn't pay attention on that field trip we took sophomore year."

Isla steps fully into my space now, bafflement parting her lips. "How could you not? That was the most informative day of the entire year!"

Of course she would get passionate about the Folk Haven Dam. One more thing I love about her.

I shrug. "I was distracted."

Some of the shock clears from her face as she nods in understanding. "By the beauty of it? I missed the first five minutes of the tour because I was staring at the structure in its entirety. But I found the guide before we got on the bus and asked her to repeat what I'd missed. You should have done that."

The guide would've needed to repeat the entire speech because Isla was wearing a white button-up shirt and a plaid skirt that day. My horny teenage mind couldn't stop playing out schoolgirl fantasies. Didn't help that she raised her hand every five minutes, asking some intelligent question that got my blood up.

"You could tell me about it now." *Please stay and talk to me.* "Start from the beginning. How did they even make the dam?"

Her mouth pops open, cheeks flushed, gaze sparking with excitement, her entire form thrumming as she readies to give me a lecture on dams.

But then she pauses.

Don't stop. Focus on me.

Isla shakes her head, as if hearing my thoughts. "I want to, but I can't."

So close. "Why not?"

"I need to enact a plan."

"And that plan is?"

"Secret." She smiles with an air of triumph. Proud of her ability to keep a piece of knowledge to herself.

Which only makes me want to tease it out of her more.

"Can I help with your secret plan?"

Isla examines me, as if I'm a potentially handy tool, and I can imagine her working through scenarios in her head. Ways to use me. Does she have any idea how badly I want to be used?

Leave her alone. You've done enough to mess up her life.

As the guilt begins to bite at my gut, her words distract me. "You can remark on how attractive I look in my bathing suit."

Damn this woman. How can she be so honest yet always surprising?

"You want me to objectify you?"

Isla frowns, and even that expression has me mesmerized. "Only when you have my permission. Which you currently do."

She's serious. Of course she's serious. Isla almost always is.

"You have permission to objectify me too." I make the offer just to see if I can get her to blush.

I should've known better.

"Is there someone in attendance you'd like me to speak to about the attractiveness of your body in a bathing suit?" Isla scans the party, somehow thinking there's anyone here I'm more interested in than her.

"Before I can admit that, I need to know what you'll say." The light teasing in my tone hides how much I want to hear what she has to say.

Isla turns back to me, and I shiver as her gaze travels the length of my body.

There's that blush. A small reddening along her cheekbones. "I would say that the blue of your suit pairs with the blue of your eyes."

I glance down at my swim trunks, not able to hide my grin. "You think so? What else?"

Isla steps back, intently studying me, and I try to flex my muscles without noticeably putting effort in.

"I would point out your farmer's tan."

"You—my what?" I glance at my arms and realize there is a line across each bicep, denoting where my T-shirt normally sits. My chest is also a few shades paler than my forearms. "How is that attractive?" Unless it isn't and Isla's just being baldly honest about my good and bad characteristics.

"It means you are outside a lot but wearing a shirt, which means you are likely working. Probably something that involves manual labor, which is a fact supported by the muscles in your arms, chest, and"—Isla strolls around behind me—"back." She returns to face me. "And because you have less sun exposure here"—her hands indicate my middle—"you are less likely to develop skin cancer in close proximity to your vital organs. Which reminds me." She digs through a floppy bag hanging off her shoulder, coming out with a colorful tube. "Have you properly applied sunscreen? This one is reef safe. I'm aware we don't have reefs in Lake Galen, but the aquatic life could be affected by chemicals."

My mind struggles to keep up while also permanently recording everything she said about my body to memory.

"Finn?" Isla says my name, and all I want is for her to do it again.

"Hmm?"

"Do you need sunscreen?"

"Sure."

She nods. "I do too." Then, with no fanfare at all, Isla sets her drink on the dock, drops her bag beside it, and strips off her sundress, leaving her in a polka-dot two-piece fit for a pinup model.

"That suit is perfect on you," I blurt before realizing my mouth is moving.

"Good. Just like that. Maybe louder next time."

At Isla's comments, I remember that she asked for compliments.

Then, she starts to apply sunscreen to herself, and the precise movements should not turn me on as much as they do. But that's what this woman does to me.

"I am not flexible enough to evenly apply it on my back. Will you help me?" Isla extends the sunscreen, and she might as well be offering me a gold bar with the way my hands reach to eagerly snatch the thing.

When Isla turns around, I almost swallow my tongue. But, God, the way the suit cups her ass should be illegal.

You've seen her in a swimsuit before. Get yourself together.

Growing up, I spent plenty of time swimming at this house with the MacNamaras. Isla often joined, with her being a close neighbor. I drooled over her then too. But now, she has a woman's body. Fuller and softer.

And the normally standoffish woman is asking me to touch her.

I won't mess it up.

Affecting as much detachment as I can muster, I coat my palms with the white lotion and start on her shoulders. Warm under my touch, Isla's muscles relax with each pass of my hands.

I'm doing her a favor as a friend, I remind myself as I work to cover lower. *Keeping her safe in the hot sun.*

That's the thought that helps me finish the task with determination rather than lust. Keeping Isla safe. I never want her hurt again.

When I get the lowest exposed point, just above the high waist of her suit, my fingers feel the way her smooth skin turns rough in one area. The edge of a scar.

A stark reminder of why I am the last person who deserves to touch Isla.

"Do you need help?" Her voice makes me want to close my eyes, so I can listen to only her.

"Yes." *In so many ways.*

Isla turns abruptly, grabbing the sunscreen and circling around to my back. There's the unattractive squirting sound the bottle makes and the slick noise of her rubbing her hands together.

Then, she's touching me.

If only I had a railing or table to grip and brace myself. I'm worried my knees might give out.

Isla covers every inch from my shoulders to my hips, rubbing vigorously, pressing the protection into my skin. And of course, she's thorough, sneaking her fingers under the edge of my waistband to coat the parts of me that might be exposed if the material shifts around.

Go further, I silently beg.

Instead, I cup my hands over my groin to hide my body's reaction to her touch.

"That should last for the next few hours, but it is always smart to reapply multiple times a day," Isla announces, as if reading off the bottle. "I'm going to swim."

Before I can turn to thank her, she's already tossed the bottle onto her bag and executed a perfect dive off the dock. When her head pops out of the water, she's a good fifty feet away. The distance seems impossible with how quickly she reappeared.

But the woman is a selkie, so I'm not surprised.

3

ISLA

I FLOAT FAR ENOUGH beneath the surface of the murky water that no one above can see me.

But I can see them. Selkies have superior eyesight in the water, even in our human forms, and I use it now to watch one man.

Unfortunately for my plans, that man isn't Owen.

My future mate disappeared about an hour ago, taking Ramona out on a set of Jet Skis. When I realized he had gone, I decided to stay in the water. Let the cool embrace calm the unfamiliar tension that tightened my chest when Finn put his hands on me.

When I handed him my SPF 70, I braced for the discomfort of his touch. Coming into contact with people has always grated against the delicate edges of my nerves. But Finn's steady movements didn't irritate me the way I'd expected. Instead, a heady flush rose throughout my body.

Unsettling but not necessarily unpleasant.

Now, with the cool water all around me, I'm balanced again,

even as I stare up at a butt in a blue suit sticking through the hole of an inner tube.

Why do I want to bite that butt?

The thought has me remembering an old game us selkies used to play, inspired by the movie *Jaws*. Finn played, too, but the human was never very good at it. The human was always fascinated by how long Owen and I could hold our breath underwater. Of course, the two of us never stayed under so long to offer real suspicion.

I should probably surface soon. I've been down here for at least five minutes. If any of the human guests think I've drowned, the whole party will search for me. The idea of that attention tenses my muscles.

Still, I'm not ready to give up my observation of Finn's posterior.

Why do I always focus on him?

Maybe the gods believe he can help me woo my mate.

I ponder the idea of spending more time around Finn. Showing him the areas of myself that a partner might find appealing, so he can pass that knowledge on. Finn has been Owen's best friend since high school, and now, they co-own a recycling company. He is in the perfect position to talk about my positive traits to my future mate.

This is a good plan.

Stealthily, I approach the surface, and when I am just underneath the man, I give a strong kick, popping up beside him and grabbing hold of his inner tube.

"Shark attack!" I yell and then tip Finn and his shocked face straight into the lake. As he flounders for a moment, I claim the tube, heaving myself onto the slick surface and reclining on the floaty. Lying there, I let the late afternoon sun dry the droplets from my skin.

"You got me." Finn grins, treading water at my side.

"I'm much sneakier than you."

I could always tell when he was trying to creep up on me when we were younger. Sometimes, I'd let him catch me, just to hear his triumphant, booming laugh.

Finn shifts to float on his back, giving his limbs a rest. Humans don't have the same stamina in the water as we selkies do. When I spy goosebumps forming on his skin, I use the small power I have over water to coax warmer currents to surround him. No reason for Finn to be cold just because I'm better at the shark attack game than he is.

Recalling his question from earlier, I let a wave of hope rise in my chest. "Do you still want to hear about dams?"

Finn perks up. "Yes. But only if I can hang on to the tube while you talk."

"Acceptable."

He crosses his arms on top of the rubbery surface and rests his chin on their pillow as his body relaxes.

"The first thing that needs to happen when building a dam is temporarily redirecting the river. This means creating a diverting tunnel ..."

As I detail the step-by-step process of how the Folk Haven Dam was constructed, Finn keeps his eyes on my face the entire time. I'm about to start on recent updates when a shout grabs our attention.

"Hey! Finn! Isla! Burgers are ready."

Glancing over, I realize that Owen was the one yelling.

When did he get back? And when did the sun start to set?

"How long have I been talking?" I turn to look at Finn, who's still staring at me.

"Not sure. Lost track of time. You hungry?"

At the hollowness in my stomach, I realize I am. "Yes."

With a quick move, I fold my body and slip through the inner hole of the tube, sinking into the water, only to surface next to Finn.

"You distracted me," I inform him.

The man grins before swimming toward the dock, towing the water toy behind him with one arm.

When we rejoin the party, I accept another drink from Moira—this one, a hard seltzer. The bubbles zing in a pleasant way against my throat, easing a soreness I didn't realize was there. I must have talked for a long time. With so much noise going on now in this larger group, I don't get the urge to speak. I gather my food and settle on a bench roughly built from a tree trunk. Ready to observe, telling myself to focus on Owen and figure out the best way to earn his lifelong devotion.

Normally, I would not approve of the idea of pursuing a man who hasn't shown much, if any, interest. But there is a key component that makes our situation different.

Fate.

Well-known lore among selkies states that we will identify our mate when they save us from great danger. When I was sixteen, I almost died. Owen rescued me that terrifying night, and once I recovered from the experience, I realized the weight of his actions. The gods had spoken, and I listened as intently as anyone with true respect for their divine power would.

Owen would be my mate.

Of course, I was a child then, with plenty of life goals I wanted to achieve without the burden of matehood. So, I put it off. For a few years.

For fourteen years. I might have gone for fifteen if it wasn't for the way my last relationship ended. The man had cried. A lot. Because he thought we were going to spend the rest of our lives together and I only wanted the occasional sexual partner. After escaping that emotional display, I admitted the day had come to date the man fate had provided for me.

Today is that day. Or at least, the start of it. Because I am not the type of woman to shove someone out of the way to declare my intentions. I would rather Owen realize I am here and that we are destined to be together and then come willingly.

Eagerly would be preferred.

I'd opt for a mate to be excited about our pairing rather than resigned to it. Advice I might need to apply to myself now that I consider the idea.

I cannot say that I am particularly energetic about the idea of being with Owen.

He's a good man. A good friend. He'll make a good mate.

All of that is ... good.

I like good, I remind myself.

As the sky darkens, people gather on the shore and the dock to watch the sun set over the trees. I spot Calder walking hand in hand with a woman exactly how he described, and I'm satisfied to know he found her. Once the light fades, partygoers either start to head home or settle around a fire Moira built in the large firepit.

I stay. The shrinking size of the group helps with my comfort level, and I still have a mission to complete. Not that I expect I'll make much headway tonight as I watch Owen pull Ramona into his lap in an Adirondack chair across the way.

The size of this hill I need to climb to claim him only seems to grow, and I stifle a sigh.

A presence that is somehow warmer than the flames settles in the open space next to me on my tree bench.

Finn. The name, even as I think it, flows through me. Filling me up.

He holds out his plate. "Want one?"

Finn offers brownies. And pretzels.

"Is this a coincidence, or did you remember?" I pick up one of the gooey chocolate treats and carefully arrange pretzels on top before biting down. Soft, sweet, salty, crunchy.

The perfect dessert.

"I pay attention," he murmurs.

I nod in approval.

"Isla." Sorcha crouches by my side. "I wanted to let you know we have a free bed if you want to stay over."

"Thank you. I'll consider it."

The kind woman squeezes my shoulder before strolling off.

Staying over at the MacNamaras' was one of my favorite things when I was younger. I'd watch movies late into the night with everyone and then gorge on the delicious breakfast Mr. MacNamara made in the morning. The offer appeals to me as much as it used to because it means a break from my parents and their endless rules.

I love the two people who raised me more than I love the gods themselves. Unfortunately, Ann and Patrick Brown are rigid. They have many fears, most related to the possibility of our discovery. The human world would cause quite a commotion if everyone found out about mythical creatures, and my parents have outlined every gruesome outcome in detail to me.

I appreciate their candor, and I know I get much of my practical manner from them. But I find I am not ruled by the same worries they are. Aware of them, of course. I am cautious when not around my kind. But, while I might not enjoy large gatherings, I do like being around people different than me even if some things get lost in translation.

Moira, Folk Haven's premier—and only—real estate agent, is helping me find a piece of land to purchase. Houses tend to pass down through generations, and I don't want to wait around for my parents to pass away to have a home of my own.

If my mother lectures me about properly locking my car again, I might set up a tent on a piece of land rather than wait around for a house to be built.

Sorcha's offer of a night away from their hovering is welcome.

Unfortunately, I won't be able to accept.

"Are you staying over?" Finn asks before picking up his own brownie and taking a hearty bite.

"Likely not."

He swallows his dessert. "Why not?"

Despite my normal habit of honesty, I hesitate before sharing. The truth is, I don't enjoy people knowing how I lose control.

But Finn waits patiently as I convince myself there is no reason to be ashamed.

"I often have nightmares if I don't follow a certain routine before bed," I admit. "I'd rather not wake people up with my screaming."

"Screaming?" He leans closer, his shoulder pressing against mine. "Those must be bad."

I nod. Things often are when they're based on actual trauma.

The pressure of his body against mine is nice. Soothing. I lean into him as well.

"There's no way to re-create your routine here?" he asks.

If only I'd packed the proper supplies. I frown down at my towel bag before shaking my head. "The most important part is relieving stress. Which I do by providing myself with two to three orgasms."

There's a choking sound, and I glance over to find Finn coughing. I get up, hurrying over to a cooler with drinks, and grab him a bottle of water. When I hand it off, he downs half the thing in two swallows.

"Thank you," he rasps. Then, he drinks some more as I return to my spot beside him. After finishing the bottle, the human continues, "So"—he clears his throat—"orgasms, huh?"

"Yes." The carbonation of my seltzer diminishes with each moment, and I set it to the side. "I was relieved when I found out they worked. But I can only ever manage one with my hand. I need a vibrator to get more, and I didn't bring one with me." As honest as I am with my parents, I don't know that I want to return home to grab a self-stimulator, only to immediately head back out.

With Finn quiet beside me, I realize I must have overshared. I tend to mix up what is and what is not acceptable to discuss in relation to sex.

Maybe I should place him in the same category as my parents.

But that doesn't seem right. "I apologize if I made you uncomfortable."

"What about with a partner?" His question isn't one I expected.

"A partner?"

Finn stares into my eyes, focusing on me in the method he seems to have perfected, coaxing me to float forever in those gray-blue depths. "Has a partner ever gotten you to more than one orgasm?"

Blinking away from his hypnotizing stare, I consider my past liaisons. "One. But that was because he was a particular fan of cunnilingus."

Finn goes quiet again.

Since I don't have anything further to add to the conversation, I stretch my toes toward the fire, enjoying the way my skin tingles in the heat. A scent drifts past my nose. A cedarwood soap, mixed with the earthy smell of lake water. Must be Finn's still-damp hair.

"What if I offered to help you relax before bed?" the human asks, his voice lower than before. "Would you stay over?"

All of my nerves clench, as if I pressed as close to the fire as I could get without setting myself aflame. "Define *relax*."

"I could help you achieve your orgasms."

An image enters my head—Finn fully bare, in a bed with me.

Straining. Panting. Sweating.

I tuck my feet close to my body, suddenly overheated.

"That would not be a good idea." The words fall from my

tongue without consideration, which is not how I prefer to converse.

"Why not?"

Because I like the idea too much and you are not who the fates chose for me.

"Do you recall the plan I mentioned earlier? The secret one?"

"Yes."

"The plan is to seduce Owen. And I cannot do that while you are seducing me."

4

FINN

SHE WANTS TO SEDUCE OWEN?

Owen MacNamara?

"Why would you want to do that?"

Isla rarely shows emotions on her face, but if anything, she's gone stonier. The woman crosses her arms over her chest, grasping her opposite elbows, as if she needed to protect her inner organs.

"We're meant to be together." Her lips thin, as if she were trying to suck the declaration back into her mouth. "You wouldn't understand. It's a family thing."

Family? More like selkie.

I'd bet my half of Clean Haven Recycling that this has something to do with the society of mythical creatures Isla and Owen belong to. The one that she doesn't know I know about.

Is this some arranged-marriage type of situation? The idea has me gritting my teeth.

Not that I have any aversion to arranged marriages. My

coworker Adity has one, and she's in a loving relationship with her husband. Good for them.

My problem is with Isla Brown partnering herself off with Owen.

Could I do it? Could I watch Isla walk down the aisle with my best friend? Watch them be together for the rest of my life?

Holding hands.

Kissing.

Going off to bed together each night, where he'd ...

I might be sick.

But then I glance over at my business partner, where he's laughing, having a good time with Ramona. The guy has always been a flirt, never tied down for long by any relationship. But he's loyal as hell, and I find it strange that he's flaunting another woman in front of his supposed future partner.

So, maybe it's not a set-in-stone arrangement, but Isla seems to think Owen and she should be a match, and that's what I don't get.

"Does he know you're trying to seduce him?"

Isla glances over to where Owen is whispering something in Ramona's ear, which causes the woman to chuckle.

"I haven't informed him." She averts her gaze from the couple. "I thought a natural seduction might be the best approach."

"As opposed to an unnatural seduction?" I can't help poking at her clinical wording.

Isla smooths her hands over the skirt of her sundress. Water spots linger on the floral fabric, where her damp suit presses against the material.

"You caught me. I'm unsure of the proper vocabulary to use to describe my plan. Enticing maybe." Her head tilts in thought. "Encouraging."

"Foraging," I throw out.

"What?" Her brows dip as she stares at me. "No. I'm not *foraging* for Owen. He's not a blackberry bush."

When Isla's focus is on me, all common sense leaches out of my brain, leaving only my longing in place. No memory of why I'm unworthy of her. Which has me returning to our original topic.

"Obviously, I'm not grasping your secret plan. But I think it's clear, Owen is spoken for tonight. Which means you're open to accepting other offers." *You can stop thinking about him for a few hours and see me instead.* "Do you want to stay the night here?"

Isla reaches for the last pretzel on my plate, crunching on the snack before answering. "Moira makes good mimosas. And Mr. MacNamara always cooks his bacon to the exact right amount of crispiness."

I press my lips together, not sure if I should laugh or groan at the knowledge that the breakfast offerings might determine if I get to spend the night with the woman I've wanted since freshman year of high school.

Setting aside my plate, I turn to fully face Isla, letting our knees brush. She doesn't shift away, which is her normal reaction to someone moving closer to her.

"Do you want me to give you a minimum of three orgasms?" I'm glad our bench is on the opposite side of the fire from most of the gathering. Less likely to be overheard and have a random person butt in to the conversation when they realize what we're discussing.

"You are confident you can achieve three?" She eyes my hands, as if they'd provide references.

"I don't give up easily." Leaning in to catch her gaze, I stare into the mocha irises that haunt my dreams and fantasies. "And I won't just use my fingers."

Her focus drops to my mouth, and she tips forward, as if my words had a magnetic effect on her. The same way hers always draw me in.

Then, Isla sits straight, whatever spell I was briefly able to cast broken. But before I accept the rejection, the selkie reaches a hand out, carefully pinching my index finger, brushing her thumb over the pad in a gentle caress.

"I would only need your help tonight."

One night. More than I ever hoped. More than I deserve.

"Just tonight." The words are a promise to her and a warning to myself.

Do not try for more.

Whether or not Isla continues to pursue Owen doesn't matter because she's not mine.

"I'll stay the night," she says.

Exhilaration pulses through my muscles. I want to scoop her up and sprint to the house, find the closest bedroom and worship her until the sun rises. But Isla makes no move to get up, so I stay still beside her, all quivering tension and need.

"Let me know when you're ready for bed."

5

———

ISLA

WHEN I STEP out of the bathroom in my borrowed sleep clothes, Finn is waiting for me in the hall. He's out of his swim trunks, dressed in athletic shorts and a T-shirt. Covering up his farmer's tan.

Disappointment trickles through me at finding him so thoroughly dressed. Which is an illogical reaction. It's not as though he needs to take any of his clothes off for what we're about to do.

"I won't just use my fingers."

What that simple sentence did to me should be a crime. All my functions and thoughts were sent into a flailing mess, just like when I tipped him from his inner tube.

I need to reestablish control over the situation. This is one night. A service between friends. There can't be anything more. Proven by my parents' response when I texted to let them know they shouldn't expect me home tonight.

Mom: *Be careful. We've heard the MacNamaras invite humans to their parties. If you feel unsafe, call us, and we'll come pick you up.*

If only they knew what *I've* invited a human to do. But there's no reason to share that piece of information.

As I approach Finn now, he watches me with those blue-gray eyes. But that's not new.

I pass by him, reaching for the door to the bedroom I was assigned. Pushing it open, I turn to face a still-waiting Finn.

"Ready?"

"Are you?" he asks back, falling into his habit of answering me with questions.

And I fall into mine of answering with the truth. "Yes."

In fact, I've been ready for years.

Just because I know that being intimate with Finn could never lead to anything permanent doesn't mean I've never thought about it. When I touch myself before bed each night, he is the most common partner I picture myself with. Fantasies of slowly peeling off that damp red shirt he wore in the line to get coffee three years ago. Having him bite me instead of the bear claw he ordered. The two of us disappearing into Coffee & Claws's single-user restroom, where he would press me up against a wall and drive into me.

Outside of my head, I would never approve of a public restroom as a sexual environment, but in my dreams, every surface is as sanitary as I need it to be.

All this to say, yes, I am ready for the real thing.

The true question is, will I be ready tomorrow morning to never let this happen again?

He precedes me through the door, which I close and lock behind me. Finn halts in the middle of the room, staring at the bed.

"Who's in charge here?" he asks.

The possibilities cycle through my mind. "You, but I maintain veto rights. And we're agreed that the goal is two orgasms."

"Three," he corrects. "At a minimum."

"Three," I agree because he seems confident. "Where would you like me?"

Finn jerks his chin toward the bed. "Sit on the edge."

I make sure not to slouch as I settle on the mattress and briefly wonder if good posture assists in achieving orgasms. I'm about to pose this question out loud when I meet Finn's stare.

There's some intense emotion on his face, but I always have trouble reading feelings from faces.

This one is starvation, maybe?

"Are you hungry?" I ask. "There were still plenty of brownies. I could get you one."

Finn closes his eyes, and I become fascinated with the long sweep of his lashes. What an impressive sweep. I'd like to measure the curvature. Can protractors be used on lashes?

"That's not what I'm hungry for." His voice rumbles between us.

"There was pie too."

Finn laughs, a small puff of breath, before stepping toward me. When we're both standing, Finn is only a handful of inches taller than I am. But now, he looms, towering, his dark hair flopping over his brow as he gazes down at me.

"Where can I touch you?"

Interesting. I assumed he would focus entirely on my vulva, but Finn's eyes trail over more than the space between my legs.

"Neck down." I decide, suddenly worried he might try to kiss me. That would do things to my brain I can't even contemplate.

He nods. "I plan to use my hands and my mouth and tongue."

"Yes. Fine. Good." I shake my head, realizing how my rapid-fire words paired with his statement. "I didn't mean those to match up, as in your mouth is only fine. I'm sure your mouth is exceptional. I amend my response to amazing, exceptional, fantastic."

Finn kneels in front of me, pressing his fists to the bed on either side of my hips. The muscles in his forearms strain, making his scar stand out against his pale skin. I catch sight of his wide smile before he leans in to trace his lips along my collarbone. The highest spot I've allowed him.

There's less air in the room. I'm unsure how that's scientifically possible, but a moment ago, I was breathing fine, and now, I can't seem to locate the oxygen.

"Let's take this off." Finn grips the bottom of my shirt, easing the material up and over my head. "Isla," he groans my name.

"What?" I stare between the T-shirt Moira lent me and my bare chest. "I'm going to bed after this. I don't wear a bra to bed."

Finn sits back on his heels, staring. Again. Always staring.

"Are you formulating a strategy?" Maybe I should have provided notes on my pleasure areas prior to this starting.

The human reaches forward, warm hands clasping my sides while his thumbs press just under the curves of my chest. Finn holds my body in his determined grasp, as if he plans to lift me or pull my torso toward his. And all the while, he stares, nostrils flaring, breaths unsteady.

Oh good. I'm not the only one experiencing oxygen issues.

Without warning, Finn dives forward, latching on to my nipple and sucking the bud into his mouth. A storm forms in my body, originating from the single tip of my breast. Pleasure and wildness crash through me.

"Where can I touch you?" I gasp the question, berating myself for not asking sooner.

He lets go with a pop. "Anywhere. Everywhere." The two words brush hot against my nipple, and then he returns to his suction, and I dig my fingers into his messy, damp hair.

Finn spends a stretch of time with my breasts, plumping them with his hands, licking and teasing my nipples. The hurricane of ecstasy he creates rolls downward to between my legs. He's stimulating me without even removing my bottoms. When his lips offer another strong tug, I can't help whimpering and rubbing my thighs together, craving friction.

"Spread your knees," Finn commands, even as his grip digs into my thighs, guiding my legs apart.

Losing the small bit of pressure drags an insensible note of protest from my throat. Then, the man settles his body in the newly made space, and with a hand on my behind, Finn drags me to the very edge of the bed. Suddenly, my aching middle is pressed flush against his abdomen.

"Oh. I like that." Eagerly, I wrap my legs around his torso, grinding against him.

"Can you come like this?" Finn's lips brush the hard tip of my nipple with each word, sending small splashes of pleasure through my body. But I want the massive crashing waves from a moment ago.

"I've never tried. If you suck on me hard like before, I think I can."

Finn groans deep and then locks his lips around my areola, pulling, tugging, and meanwhile, I rock my hips against him. Then, he bites gently yet still hard enough for a sting. The shift in sensations surprises me. Suddenly, an orgasm rolls through my muscles.

With a hiccup, I collapse back on the bed, limbs both loose and pulsing. My legs fall open, releasing their hold on his trim waist.

"One." Finn grins down at me.

I meet his eyes over the length of my heaving chest.

Gods, he might get me to three.

The talented human leans in to press a kiss against my breastbone and then again an inch lower, and he continues tracing a trail down my belly until he reaches my waistband.

"Can I?"

"Yes."

He hooks his thumbs in my shorts and underwear, sliding the fabric down my legs. There's a pause, and I realize Finn stopped touching me. Propping myself up onto my elbows, I realize he's staring again.

"You have a tattoo," he murmurs.

"I do." Reaching to my hip, I finger the neatly drawn lines permanently imprinted on my skin. "It's the Tower Bridge in London. Did you know I went to London?"

Finn shakes his head.

"I visited on my own a few years ago." An adventure I never told my parents about. They likely would have had mutual panic attacks if they'd discovered I was on a different continent than my selkie skin for two weeks. But I don't tell them everything in my life, which the tattoo is a constant reminder of.

"Must have been a good trip if you got a tattoo." Finn continues to examine the detailed image the artist spent four hours sketching into my flesh with her needle.

The picture is beautiful, but it's not going to contribute to my orgasm. I sit all the way up.

"Do you find tattoos unattractive?" My fingers spread, obscuring the image. "I might be able to achieve another orgasm on my own, if you'd prefer to stop."

I didn't think to warn him beforehand. The possibility that Finn might be turned off by the piece of art I love so much has me wanting to crawl under the covers. But as I move to shift away, he clutches my hips.

"Beautiful," he rasps. "The tattoo. You. I want—" The sentence doesn't finish with a word but instead an action. Finn dives between my thighs, pressing a hot, openmouthed kiss to my core.

Sensitive from the first orgasm, I can't help a yelp of surprise, but then I have my hands buried in the silky strands of his hair, squirming as he licks up and down my vulva lips.

"Gods!" my voice squeaks when he brushes my clitoris.

After the treatment my nipples received, I'm almost scared for him to keep going.

But I'm more terrified he'll stop.

The first suck has my thighs shaking.

The second overwhelms my toes, curling them painfully tight.

I brace for a third, but he pauses.

"Can I penetrate you with my finger?"

"Yes!" The word comes out as a sob. "Please," I beg.

"How many?"

"As many as you have!"

He chuckles against my clit. But I can't explain to him that I've become so lost in his touches that I can't remember how many fingers a human has.

Is it the same as me? How many do I have?

I don't care.

Then, a pressure enters me. In wonder, I gaze down, watching Finn ease his touch in and out of my vagina, his skin growing slick with my pleasure. His chin tilts up until our stares meet.

"For me?" he whispers.

My shaking hands cradle his head. "Finn." His name is my breath. I survive off him.

Gray-blue eyes grow dark as a storm, but they don't leave mine as he bends forward to take my clit between his lips. This time, when he sucks, his fingers curl inside me.

And I let him watch as the second, larger wave rushes through me.

Two.

6

———

FINN

ISLA WILL ORGASM a third time if I die trying. And who knows? Maybe I am dead and was a decent enough guy in life that I'm in heaven. Because I can't imagine a better paradise than the space between this woman's legs.

But that can't be right. I was never good enough for her.

The only thing that would make this better is if I could ease the ache in my cock. Which definitively shows I'm not in heaven because I'm obviously a selfish bastard.

Still, I take a chance.

"Isla?"

Her head lolls to the side, eyes hazy as she gazes down at me. My heart hurts with how gorgeous she is, lying here, lax from the pleasure I've given her.

"Finn," she says my name like it's the answer. Just like she did a moment ago when I thought I'd break in half from wanting her.

"Do you mind if I touch myself while I take care of your number three?"

Slowly, she sits up. "You're aroused?"

Pretty much since the moment I saw her in that high-waisted swimsuit. "Yes."

"Let me see."

Curious what she'll do, I stand up. The tent in my shorts is impossible to ignore.

"I would prefer your clothes off." The selkie stares intently at my erection, which only gets me harder.

"Whatever you want." And I mean it. If she asked me to dig my still-beating heart out from under my rib cage, I'd do it for her. I tug my shirt off, then drop my shorts, and kick them away.

"I want to be in charge now." Isla digs her teeth into her lower lip, and my dick pulses at the move.

"Go for it."

My breaths come in short bursts as she rises off the bed. When Isla steps in close, my tip brushes her belly, leaving a drop of pre-cum on her skin. The sight and sensation drag a needy sound from deep in my chest.

Isla scoops up my hand and steps around me, giving enough of a tug that I realize she wants me to pivot. I rotate with her, ready for more direction.

"I'm in charge," she murmurs, as if I need reminding.

"I'll do anything you want."

The woman shoves my chest hard, so I topple backward on the bed. Before I can move, Isla brings her hands down on my thighs. That touch has me groaning. But then the temptress crawls over me, centering herself where my hard dick lies against my stomach.

"Don't worry, Finn." She pats my pec, and my muscles twitch in frantic anticipation. "I'll get number three."

"But I—holy fuck." The curse spills out in response to Isla lowering herself onto my hips, sandwiching my aching cock between my stomach and her hot pussy.

She draws more expletives from me as she begins to rock, rubbing her slick core along my length.

Using me the way I always wished she would.

The ecstasy forms a hazy fog over my mind, demanding I simply experience the sensations. That I allow myself to sink into nerve endings and become a beast of only physical touch.

But I battle that urge. As much as I crave this pleasure, more than anything, I want to remember. To sear every moment of this time with Isla into my brain, so I'll never forget, even when years have passed since this night.

My eyelids grow heavy, but I force them open, cataloging the rhythm of her hips and the angles she sways them. Noting the exact pitch of each of her gasps, cherishing the few guttural grunts when a certain spot presses into me. I cup her swaying tits, measuring the curve with my hands. Isla's nipples taunt me, the peaks still hard and flushed from my earlier attention. I rear up, capturing one point in my lips, desperate to savor the flavor of her skin.

Mistake. At my first lick, she cries out, body curling around mine, riding through her orgasm.

Her third bout of pleasure.

I never want this to end, but Isla bears down hard as her fingers tangle in my hair. With her pressed against me, the heat of our bodies mixing until we're one, I can't stop my rolling wave, and the crest crashes through me. Out of me.

My groan is half-pleasure, half-pain, and I jerk as I spill in the space between us, my orgasm throwing up a barrier.

"Three," Isla murmurs against my neck, her voice sleepy. Already, she's fading, just as she promised.

I've fulfilled my role, but I can't let her go. Can't admit that this brief, perfect moment is finished. That I got all I can ever have from her.

"You should sleep here," the selkie mumbles, resting her head on my shoulder.

"You don't mind?" Good thing she's so out of it because I struggle to mask the desperate hope in my voice.

Isla slowly shakes her head. "Thank you for helping with the nightmares." Her voice is barely audible as she nestles closer to me. "Hate to dream of drowning."

Guilt tears through me, ripping apart the joy and glow of this night.

Isla has nightmares about drowning.

And it's my fault.

As I try to focus on the memory of her pleasured sounds, another recollection shoves to the front of my mind. The hard thunk of a boat propeller hitting an object just before a scream of pain.

Carefully, I lay Isla down on the covers. She barely stirs, already asleep. I retreat to the bathroom, where I wash my cum off my torso and then wet a hand towel before returning to the bedroom. With gentle strokes, I wipe Isla's stomach, taking special care around her tattooed hip even though she's long healed.

Beneath the ink, I can still see the twist and pucker of skin she tried to cover with her beautiful image. The scar that I caused.

I should leave. The slightly decent part of my brain reasons. *I don't deserve to be near her.*

But then a louder, more selfish part roars an opinion. *She told me to stay!*

Grabbing a quilt off the foot of the bed, I spread the patterned blanket over Isla and then slip under the cover. Without encouragement, she turns into my body. This woman, averse to most physical touch when awake, seeks to plaster every inch of her naked body against mine while she sleeps.

I hold her close, wishing that what we just shared could eradicate my dark memories.

But as Isla sleeps, content, my mind drags me back to that night.

I dived into chill waters, searching for the owner of the pained sound. In the darkness, I felt a large, slippery form and dragged the mass to shore. In the muted light cast from a nearby house, I stared down in horror at a twisted creature that resembled a clumsy attempt at melding the human body with an animal's. The mouth that gasped in pain belonged to Isla, the girl I could never take my eyes off during classes.

How could she have been that thing?

Then, I saw the blood. A jagged gash on the part of her body that was other. Despite the odd form, I desperately pressed my hands to the torn flesh and tried to get my brain to work.

Next thing I knew, another water creature crawled onto the shore. As I watched in horrified fascination, the seal-like being dug its clawed flippers into its chest, and a moment later, my best friend shucked off the skin, as if the animal form were a costume.

"Owen?" I choked on his name.

"I'll explain later." All his focus was on the creature under my hands. "What happened to Isla?"

"It is her?"

Then, she shuddered and moaned, and I set aside my questions.

Owen did something, peeling away the strange parts of her body until she was simply an injured, naked girl under my hands. The sight was somehow worse.

"What do we do?" I looked to my friend, hoping he'd have the answers I didn't.

Owen's face, normally relaxed and teasing, was stone. He clutched two shimmering cloaks, which I later learned were Isla's and his selkie skins.

"You have your keys?" he asked.

Daring to remove one bloody hand from Isla's wound, I fished the keys out of my back pocket. Owen snatched them and took off at a sprint, the two glimmering pelts slung over his shoulder.

"Meet me at the road!" he yelled.

I managed to wrap my shirt around Isla's waist as a poor attempt at a bandage before lifting her in my arms and carrying her to the road. Owen tore toward us in my rusty car. I slid into the backseat, Isla cradled against my chest. She began to shake, letting out pained whimpers.

"Hospital?" I asked, mentally cursing the forty-minute drive to the nearest one.

Owen shook his head, speeding down the twisty back roads. "There's someone closer."

I thought he meant a local doctor.

But Owen took us to someone else. My knowledge of the world expanded in a lot of ways that night.

Isla was unconscious the entire time though. Once she was fixed up as could be, Owen sat me down. Told me about selkies. Then, he made it clear how hard my life would become—and Isla's too—if I repeated anything about the night.

I easily agreed to keep my mouth shut. Gladly.

Selfishly.

Because a naive me believed Isla's injury was all that needed to heal.

Turns out, I scarred more than her body that night.

7

ISLA

I NEVER IMAGINED myself as a snuggler. But then I wake up, tucked in Finn's arms, and have to recalibrate the view I have of myself. With this man so close, my body responding to every rise and fall of his chest, there's an insistent push for me to alter multiple ways I approach my life.

For example, my idea of partnering with any person besides this perfect human.

This is what I've always imagined it would feel like to lie next to my mate.

But Finn *isn't* my mate.

I need to find Owen and transfer this longing to him.

There's a sudden pressure behind my eyes, and a moment later, tears start to flow down my cheeks.

Wrong, a voice shouts inside of me, but I can't solve the puzzle. I don't know where the piece fits. Where I fit.

Finn sleeps heavy enough that I successfully slide out of his hold without him waking.

But the minute I'm free, I want his arms to capture me again. My body still hums from what we did last night.

All I want is to wake him up and see if we can surpass three.

Instead, I remind myself of the dictate the gods gave me all those years ago. But their divine voices have never been quieter. I pull on the borrowed sleep clothes I didn't end up wearing to bed and leave the room. Downstairs, wonderful sweet and savory smells waft from the kitchen, and I find most of the MacNamara clan up and eating along with a few more guests.

"Morning, honey." Sorcha offers me a relaxed smile while she waits by the French press. "Fill your plate. There's plenty to go around."

"Thank you. Am I the last one up?" I already know the answer is no, seeing as how I just left Finn in my bed. But in my initial scan of the room, I didn't spot Owen.

She glances around. "Still a few stragglers behind you. I told everyone they should sleep in. Didn't stop Owen and Ramona from getting on the road before the sun was up."

My hand freezes over a stack of waffles. "On the road?"

Sorcha nods, covering a yawn with her hand. "They're driving down to Key West for the week. Wanted to avoid traffic best they could."

He's gone.

The man I am fated to mate is gone. Drove off with another woman. Probably going to have a week full of unending orgasms together.

I should sigh.

I should be frustrated.

I should be jealous.

Instead, I'm relieved. As I work my way around the counter, gathering more food, I poke at the emotion, wondering why my heart can't follow the gods' simple dictate.

Fall in love with the person who saves you.

Aka Owen MacNamara. The man who pulled me from the

water after I was clipped by a boat propeller and almost drowned. Or bled to death. There were lots of life risks he saved me from that night.

I crunch on a salty strip of bacon as I gaze out of the house's panoramic windows, overlooking the sprawling waters of Lake Galen. The gentle, glittering waves bring clarity.

Maybe Owen has the right of it.

What's the rush? We could wait another year. Another ten. Absence makes the heart grow fonder, right?

And in the meantime, I can pursue other things.

My mind continues churning as I head toward the stairs, balancing my breakfast plate in one hand.

When I play with the idea of partnering myself to Owen ten years from now, the deadline still looms too close.

How about never?

I pause with my hand on the knob of the bedroom door, experiencing another rush of relief at that thought.

I don't need a mate.

What's the point, really? A partner for life might sound good on paper, but I've done fine on my own.

So, no, I don't need a mate.

I don't need Owen MacNamara.

What I need is …

I need …

"Gods." I'm not sure if I'm speaking to them or cursing them. "I need Finn."

For however long he agrees, we'll have … something.

This lack of a plan is disconcerting, but the one piece I do have—Finn—is absolutely right. I also have determination as I push through the door and stride up to the bed, where the human in question still sleeps, snoring softly. His lips are parted, emitting the cute noise.

I settle on the bed at his side, waiting for him to realize I'm here.

He doesn't.

Tired of waiting on him, I take charge.

"I want to kiss you," I announce.

Finn jerks awake, eyes wild as he stares around the room, his attention finally landing on where I sit, cross-legged beside him.

"Isla?"

"After you brush your teeth, I want to kiss you." I extend a piece of bacon. "If it wasn't clear, I'm doing away with the *neck down only* rule I established last night."

Finn blinks at me, his long, fascinating lashes brushing his cheeks with every downward stroke. He doesn't answer.

"Are you still waking up, or are you trying to find a nice way to tell me you don't want to kiss me?" Maybe if I maintain my normal detached demeanor, the second response won't hurt as much.

"I want to kiss you." His quick reply eases a tension in my chest I didn't want to admit to.

"You can eat first." I hold out my plate of assorted food offerings. "There's more downstairs. Best get your strength up. I want a vigorous make-out session. Possibly more orgasms. We can discuss it."

With a slow-moving hand, as if he expects me to yell *shark attack* and dump the breakfast in his lap, Finn reaches out and retrieves a slice of avocado, swallowing the piece in one bite. He shifts to mirror my seated position, keeping the sheets bunched around his waist.

"You've changed your mind since last night." His fingers carefully retrieve a raspberry.

"Yes." I watch as the juicy little fruit passes through lips I want to explore.

"Are you still planning to seduce Owen?"

"Unlikely. If I do, it won't happen for another decade."

Finn's lips thin, but I still find them very kissable. "Why? You're not interested in him, are you?"

"No. I should be, but I'm not."

"Why should you be?"

"I said before, it's not something you'd understand. A family thing."

Finn gives me his hard stare, and the weight of his focus strokes along my nerve endings. "You mean, a magic thing?"

The man's question triggers an instinctual warning, the blaring bell in my head only made stronger by my parents.

He knows something.

If he knows anything, it's too much.

What did I do? What mistake did I make?

My heart rate speeds and my breath with it.

"Isla?"

My eyes flick to the door.

Should I run? The MacNamaras are just downstairs. I could tell them …

Realization crashes over me.

Finn is Owen's best friend. Coworker. Has spent countless hours in this house.

He might have learned about my kind. Many humans in Folk Haven know. But not all.

"How well do you know the MacNamaras?" I use my most neutral tone to ask the question, attempting to ease away from a panic that won't serve me.

"Very well."

"How well?"

Finn sighs, dragging a hand through his hair, which messes up the dark mass more than usual. "Well enough to know what happens the night of the dark moon."

The night of the dark moon.

His phrasing reveals the truth. That is how most selkies speak of the one night a month we decree it safe enough to bring out our second skins and take on our other form. On the pitch-black nights, with no moonlight to reveal us, we can reconnect with our animalistic selves, become one with the water, and replenish our souls.

"Owen told you."

Finn grimaces. "Yes. But only because he had to."

"You forced him?"

"No!" Finn leans toward me and then immediately back again.

Then, he stands from the bed, and I catch a glimpse of his bare ass before he pulls on his discarded shorts. Now partially clothed, he paces the floor, and I watch his movements, trying to figure out the proper reaction to this situation. Or at least come up with a question to ask that'll help me understand.

Suddenly, Finn crouches beside me, and when he speaks, the pain in his voice reverberates off my bones. "Owen told me to help me understand the extent of the harm I'd caused. Because I was there the night you were injured, Isla." He bows his head. "I'm the reason you have nightmares."

8

FINN

I DON'T KNOW if I'm doing the right thing.

But I hope I am. Hope that knowing more details about the event might in some way help Isla sleep through the night without fear.

"I was with my dad," I start, lowering myself to the floor. Placing myself beneath her.

Isla shifts until she's sitting on the edge of the bed, her feet flat on the floor. The same position she was in last night when I tasted her. It would've been so easy to kiss her this morning, but this lie has lingered between us too long.

"Your father is in prison," she points out.

"Now, he is."

A few years ago, he got wasted at a bar and punched a guy. The man pressed charges, and now, my dad is serving time for assault.

About time he got in trouble for something.

"We went out on the lake, and he brought a cooler of beers. Which was normal for him." I rub the back of my neck, not liking how that sounds like an excuse. "I just mean, it wasn't the first time he did this, and I let him get away with it. He was wasted when we headed home. After dark. The only light on the boat was out, and we couldn't see anything. I tried to get him to let me drive, but he wouldn't. I tried to get him to slow down, but he only gunned it faster. And then …" The dull thud and scream echo in my ears now.

"Your father was the one who hit me." Isla's hand presses to her hip, where the proof lies in the jagged lines of her scar.

"*We* hit you. I never should have let him drive."

The selkie eyes me, her brown gaze piercing into me, as if I were the one with a second skin she was peeling back.

Her nails dig into the covers. "You shouldn't have left me there."

"Never," I rasp. "I didn't know it was you until I pulled you out of the water. Even then, I didn't know what I was seeing. You were half and half and bleeding. But I knew your face."

Isla stares at me. "Owen pulled me from the water." Her voice wavers.

Shame tugs at my gut as I reveal the lies we offered her.

"He found us after I got you out. He took off your selkie skin and then got my car while I stayed with you. Owen drove while I tried to stop the bleeding. He took us to …" Out of everything I witnessed that night, the next bit is still the strangest.

"Madeline. A witch," she finishes.

I nod. "I thought Owen went to her house because she was the school nurse. Then, she pulled out that old book and started lighting candles and burning herbs and things. Talking in this foreign language. She healed you."

Isla slides off the bed, kneeling in front of me. I barely hold up under her focus.

"If you're going to tell me the truth, then tell me all of it." Her voice strikes me hard in the chest. "Witches don't just wave their hands and fix things."

I hang my head, chastised. "Madeline said she needed a sacrifice of the body to heal yours. I told her to take whatever she needed."

I run my thumb along the scar on my forearm, remembering the cold slice of her knife into my skin. She held my bleeding cut above Isla's wound, and where my blood touched the selkie's injury, skin slowly started knitting together.

For a time, I wondered if my blood in Isla's veins was what drew me to her. But that was a desperate man looking for a scapegoat.

Because I'd loved Isla Brown well before the accident.

"Witch's spells aren't free," the selkie insists.

I dare to meet her eyes, a rueful smile twisting my mouth. "Mowed her lawn for the rest of the summer."

Soft, piercing eyes hold mine. "You exchanged yard work to halt my death?"

All I can offer is a shrug. "It's what she asked for." I would have emptied my meager bank account. Given her my car. Hell, if the witch had demanded I be her errand boy for all eternity, I would have signed my soul over.

But she just wanted her weeds whacked.

"You were out of it the entire time and then fell asleep after the spell. I wanted to take you to your house, but Owen insisted we go to his. Because of your parents." I thought he was being ridiculous until my friend laid everything out. "How they're more worried than most about getting discovered by humans. How they'd probably pull you out of school. Maybe even move away from Folk Haven. That was when Owen told me what you all are. Not everything about you, I'm sure. But how your skins allow you to take on another form. How you only swim on the dark-moon night to keep yourselves safe. We thought you would worry less if you didn't know I was there. If only another selkie had discovered you. I promised to keep your secret." I hold out my hands, palms up, as if that'll somehow show my honesty. "We never spoke about it again after that night."

Isla's not looking at me anymore. She stares over my shoulder, but when I turn my head, all I see is a blank wall at my back. Nothing for her to be so entirely focused on.

But if she needs to zone out, then I'm not going to stop her.

I sit still, waiting. And while I wait, I catalog every inch of her, wondering if this is the last time she'll willingly be in a room with me. My gaze travels over the slope of her cheek to the bow of her lips. Lips she wanted to kiss me with. Her short hair is a bedhead mess I want to drag my fingers through. Massage her scalp until that deep V wrinkle between her brows smooths.

The large T-shirt hangs off her shoulders, hiding all her curves under its blockish cut. I'll have to rely on the shapes my hands and mouth traced last night for those memories.

Surprisingly, Isla's hands are what call to me most strongly. They sit limp in her lap, fingers relaxed. As if waiting. Waiting for my hands to slip into them, tangling our fingers, pressing palms together. Holding on to each other to stay steady through this life.

Isla's hands reanimate along with the rest of her body. She detaches her stare from the wall and stands, moving with jerky motions around the room, collecting her few items and dropping them in her bag.

All the while, I sit still.

She steps toward me and then around me, heading to the door.

"This changes things."

Then, she's gone.

9

ISLA

Finn saved me.

That fact plays on a loop in my mind as I sit at the outdated desk in my childhood bedroom.

"I'm making you tea." My mother's voice sounds through my doorway.

"Thank you, Mama."

Since she grew up in England, tea is her reaction to most problems. Not a solution. Merely a response.

Not that she knows what the problem is. I simply walked into the house and announced I'd be in my room, reevaluating my life. Both of my parents opened their mouths, no doubt ready to interrogate me about what, exactly, I meant by *reevaluate*. However, I'd exited the kitchen and jogged upstairs before they could. I'd have rather not made the announcement, but living with my parents requires some basic communication.

I need my own house.

But that's not the most important factor in my life to address at the moment.

Finn saved me.

With Owen's assistance, but it was Finn who dived into the dark water and pulled me out. Finn who tried to stop my wound from bleeding. Finn who cut himself open for the spell to heal me.

By all rights, he is my fated mate.

After the decision I made this morning to stop pursuing Owen, one might say this is a positive discovery. Instead, my mind twists, as if caught up in a whirlpool, as I struggle to understand the sudden shift.

Why did he tell me now? Does he know what saving a selkie means in our lore?

Finn's words come back to me.

"We never spoke about it again after that night."

Owen would have had no reason to tell his friend about our mating myths if the two agreed to keep Finn's involvement secret.

A small sting burns in my chest, and I realize I'm angry. Angry with Owen.

Since I was sixteen years old, the morning after that accident, Owen MacNamara has been in my future. The gods' will was clear. A traditional selkie mating was inevitable. Every long-term plan I made, Owen's shadow loomed as a required component.

But that's all he was. A shadow I let follow me around. Not concrete. Not something I longed for.

Not like Finn.

Now, when I switch out the selkie for the human, every part of my brain lights up, wanting to make plans with Finn as a necessary part of the structure. Something I should have been doing from the start.

Finn saved me.

As I imagine what the man saw, what he went through, I am in awe. That boy found an injured creature—something I have to admit must have looked nightmarish to a human. But he stayed with me. Held on to my life with his firm, unwavering grip. Then, he offered the witch whatever she demanded.

And after, more than a decade later, Finn still keeps our secret.

"Here's your tea." My mother appears before me, and I wonder if she moved quietly into my room or if I was so lost in my head that I just didn't hear her.

She pushes the hot mug into my hand. "Come tell us what changes you want to make. We'll discuss them." Then, she walks out of my room, leaving the door open, expecting me to follow.

My parents are very different than Finn's father, but I think we react to them in a similar way.

When Ann and Patrick Brown were younger, they lived in England, near the coast, swimming in the ocean on the night of the dark moon. One unfortunate time, my mother got caught in a fishing net. The experience almost killed her and left the pair with a fear of the ocean they'd once loved. So, pregnant with me and worried over the safety of their child, they moved here, to a lake in the United States mythics had started to whisper was safe for our kind.

But even in this new home, where they've lived for decades, their anxiety remains. And I have always done my best to appease them.

When Mr. Hammond shoved his son's hands away from the wheel and demanded to drive, I can easily see how Finn gave in. Just as I allowed my parents to grab hold of parts of my life I'd rather keep control of. Like the idea of who I could love.

Their fear made the idea of mating with a human seem a mountain to climb.

Maybe the difficulty of that trek is real. But if so, Finn is worth reaching the pinnacle.

Ignoring the open door, I step into my closet, choosing my

favorite dress. The one that cups my boobs almost as well as Finn's hands did last night. Only after making sure I'm as physically pleasing as I can get, I follow my mother down the stairs, finding her and my father on the back porch, each drinking their own tea.

"I need you both to get in the car and come with me," I announce, not willing to allow them an opportunity for an argument.

They stare at me. Then at each other. Then move to rise from their chairs.

One thing is certain. The Browns are unwaveringly honest about what we need.

On our way out, I grab my keys and a box from underneath the coffee table, gathering the necessary supplies required for my climb.

10

____

FINN

"You're over-mixing the batter. Give it here." My grand-mother comes to relieve me of the bowl. "What's going on behind that frown, boy? You've been a storm cloud ever since you got here. And I know it's not my baking that's made you so grumpy."

She's right. I was a swirling mess of depression long before I got home from the MacNamaras' house.

I did the right thing.

I know I did because Isla was still suffering. If she hasn't moved on from the accident, then I hope knowing more about what happened might help. Knowing the driver of the boat is off the lake, behind bars.

Of course, I'm still here. Free to torment her.

"I blew a shot with the woman of my dreams."

"The Brown girl?"

My head pops up at that, and I watch my grandmother's smug smile curl.

"Don't think I haven't seen the way you stare at her whenever she's nearby. Come on. I'm old, but I can still see."

"I didn't think I was *that* obvious." My response is all grumble.

Grandma snorts, and I'm about to smile until I'm hit with another bout of reality.

"Well, doesn't matter if the whole town knows. I messed everything up."

"Last night?"

Hell, last night. The best night of my life. Isla was in my arms, and everything was perfect.

"More like this morning. And also, years ago."

"You enjoy talking in riddles? Want me to do a puzzle to figure out what you're saying?" she scolds me while rummaging through the fridge before coming out with a stick of butter. Her long gray braid swings with each movement.

I huff out a breath. "Isla got hurt when we were younger, and I could've stopped it from happening but didn't."

Grandma barks out a laugh. "That's a lie. Biggest one I've ever heard from your mouth."

"I'm not lying!"

How does she always make me feel like I'm thirteen rather than thirty?

"Don't you raise your voice in this house."

"Sorry." I keep my voice low and steady this time, though I want to argue.

My grandmother gives me a hard look. "You're saying, you *knew* she would get hurt, and you didn't do anything?"

"No," I admit. "But I knew someone could get hurt."

"And you did nothing?"

Not after my dad shoved me away from the wheel. He would get rough sometimes after drinking too much.

"I could've done more."

My grandmother rubs the stick of butter around the inside of a metal pan. "This have anything to do with your daddy?"

"Don't see why that's relevant," I mutter.

She reaches for a wooden spoon and tries to jab my side with it as I shimmy out of her reach. "If your daddy was involved, then he was probably the one doing the hurting. And Lord knows, I was never able to control that man. So, don't go thinking you could either."

Maybe not when I was little. But by the time I was sixteen, I was just as tall and weighed almost as much. I could've wrestled the control of the boat from him. It would've been a fight, but I should've done it.

"Everything bad in the world could've been stopped if only we'd known about it first." My grandmother keeps going. "But you *don't* know beforehand. So, you can't be taking on that shame. Especially when it's your daddy doing the bad thing."

Wouldn't that be great if I didn't have to carry the guilt of that night around with me? But even if I find a way to forgive myself, that doesn't mean that Isla will suddenly appear in my life.

A loud knock sounds on the screen door.

"Got it," my grandpa announces, strolling through the kitchen with a half-empty container of seeds he was no doubt using to refill the bird feeders.

The timer goes off, and since my grandmother's hands are busy, I pull on a set of oven mitts and go to pull out the first two layers of cake. Tomorrow is my grandpa's birthday, and she prefers to get a head start on the celebration. I still need to wrap the bat box I built for their backyard. The man loves to sit on his porch every evening and listen to the squeak of the little flying creatures as they hunt for bugs in the dying light.

"Looks like we got some guests." Grandpa returns to the kitchen with a small group behind him.

When I see who the new arrivals are, I almost drop the cake tin I'm holding. I barely manage to make it to the cooling rack.

"Isla." Her name chokes from my throat.

"Finn." She steps forward, looking gorgeous in a dress that sways around her legs and hugs her chest as tightly as I want to. "These are my parents, Ann and Patrick Brown."

The two people have the same short stature, pale complexion, and dark hair color as their daughter, but only her mother has the same shade of mahogany eyes. Her dad's gaze is darker, and both of the Brown parents stare at my family as if we were a pack of wolves about to devour them.

Owen wasn't kidding when he described Isla's parents as the cautious sort.

"Nice to meet you." I move forward with slow, obvious steps, and then I hold out my hand, shaking both of their reluctant ones in turn. "These are my grandparents, Ethel and Barty Hammond." I face my family. "And you've met Isla before."

Grandma nods with a broad smile, wiping her hands on her apron. "Sure have. Why don't you all come in? Take a load off. I'll get you a cup of tea."

"Tea?" Mrs. Brown perks up at this.

"Finest sweet tea in Folk Haven," my grandpa assures them, pulling out chairs at the kitchen table.

"Of course. Sweet tea." The brief flash of hope in Mrs. Brown's face folds in on itself.

"My mother drinks hot tea," Isla announces to the room. Just as I'm struggling for a way to smooth over the misstep in Southern hospitality, Isla keeps going. "She's from England. So is my dad." Isla points at the unobtrusive man. "Hot tea is a staple for them. Did you know teatime is a huge strain on the power grids over in England? There's a surge in demand for electricity because everyone is using their electric kettle at once. I prefer sweet tea because of the high sugar content. I had yours at the town's spring picnic fifteen years ago. Finn brought me a glass. I enjoyed it but didn't understand why he was bringing me beverages. Now, I think it's because he had a crush on me."

Another silence descends over the room as Isla pauses to dig something out of her big, floppy shoulder bag, providing a respite for everyone gathered to absorb her twisting road of a speech.

I do remember that day. Isla volunteered to help build the stage for the evening musical acts, and she looked parched after hammering in all those nails. So, I brought her some tea and silently wished she'd confess how much she liked me, so I wouldn't have to shore up my pathetic teenage boy courage and ask her out myself.

Instead, she thanked me and asked that I hold her hammer while she drank.

"That's kind of you to remember my tea," my grandmother finally says, a slow smile deepening the laugh lines around her eyes. "And I have a nice selection of tea bags. A warm cup before bed always helps me sleep better."

The Brown parents offer their own hesitant smiles at that news.

"That's good. Here." Isla finally surfaces from her bag, pulling out a box. "I brought you all a puzzle." She tilts the box, so we can see the picture—*Hoover Dam, 1000 Pieces.*

"That was nice of you. Love a good puzzle." My grandfather grins, hands out to accept.

Isla passes the gift over. "I thought you four could work on that. My parents need to get out of their comfort zone and meet new people."

The Browns share a look before turning skeptical glances back on their daughter.

Isla points at them both, a warning in her eyes, as if she expects them to misbehave. "This is good for you." Then, the mythical woman turns all her piercing focus on me. "I need to speak to you."

She extends a hand, palm open, fingers spread.

Waiting for me.

As if there were any doubt that I'd take it.

I slide my hand in hers, and she pulls me through the house, out the back door. Twigs and leaves crunch under our feet as we enter the woods that separate my grandparents' house from the lake. I've stopped thinking of it as my house ever since I moved into the studio apartment above their garage, which is a separate building. There are apartments and the occasional house available for rent in town, and I can afford to buy a place of my own. But not on the lake.

And the lake always reminds me of the woman I love, so I don't want to go too far from it.

"Tell me everything you know about selkies," Isla orders after pulling me along for a stretch.

I glance back but realize she's taken us deep enough into the woods that I can't see the house anymore. Our conversation won't be overheard even if my grandparents decide to sit out on the porch.

"I know you have a second skin." Facing Isla, I meet her eyes and draw up the information Owen shared with me all those years ago. "And that you use that skin to transform into another shape. You can do that whenever you want, but the group that lives on Lake Galen mainly agreed only to turn on nights when there's no moon. Figuring the darker it is, the safer you are."

She nods, so I keep going. "I know that you are a selkie, and so are your parents. I know that Owen, Moira, Calder, Seamus, and Mrs. MacNamara are selkies, but Mr. MacNamara isn't."

When Owen first told me that, my heart tried to give me hope that I had a chance with Isla.

But that would only work if I ignored what I had done.

What your dad did, a voice in my head that sounds an awful lot like my grandmother insists.

"Owen said your parents had a bad experience and were extremely cautious. That if they found out what had happened to you and that I—a human—knew, they'd probably move you all away." That was the worst threat my friend could've thrown at me to keep my mouth shut. "I know there are others like you, but Owen didn't name names. Oh, and that the school nurse is a witch. At least, she was fourteen years ago. Ms. Madeline might have retired by now."

"What else?" Isla presses when I fall quiet.

I shake my head. "That's all I know. I mean, I can guess there's probably a textbook amount of info he didn't give me. But Owen made sure to tell me just enough to understand. And to keep quiet."

"Nothing about mates?"

Mates. The way she says the word, I can almost feel the heavy meaning behind it. And I'm suddenly ravenous for her to tell me more.

"No. I don't know anything about mates."

Isla steps forward, holding me with the power of her eyes. "Legend says a selkie will know their mate when they are saved by them."

My mind stutters over the new information. "Owen." The name pops out of my mouth, and Isla's quest to seduce the man makes more sense now. "Owen is your mate."

The guy's quick thinking is all that got us through that night. The only reason Isla is alive.

But she shakes her head. "I thought so too. Tried very hard to make my heart want him. I thought maybe if he wanted *me*, then my body would listen to what the fates had told me all those years ago."

Again, the image of my best friend holding the woman I

love invades my mind, and I squeeze my eyes shut, desperate to get rid of the sight.

"Then, I woke up this morning, next to the man I'd always wanted, and I decided that fated mates were overrated."

I blink my eyes open, staring down into her lovely, upturned face. "What are you saying?"

Isla's hands settle on my shoulders and then drag down to my chest. "I asked you to kiss me because I'd decided to stop chasing a future I thought I should want and instead pursue the one I actually craved. I was fully prepared to tell the gods they were wrong. But then you told me the truth, and I realized they weren't."

"So, you do want Owen?"

Her brows scrunch together as she stares up at me. "No. I want *you*. I've always wanted you. And it happens to be convenient that you're the one who saved my life. That you're my mate."

"Whoa. No." I move to step back, but Isla fists her hands in my shirt, holding me in place. "I'm the one who endangered you. You can't say I'm your savior when I'm the one who hurt you."

"Your father hurt me."

"I let him drive."

"Parents command a large amount of influence over their children." She sounds so reasonable, and I want to believe her.

"Looks like you can handle yours pretty well." I jerk my chin toward the house.

The selkie continues to hold me in place. "Now, I can. Because I'm a grown woman." Isla traces my face with her gaze. "Would you let your father drive intoxicated now?"

"No way. Never again."

"And I won't let my parents' fear of humans keep me from the person I need in my life."

"Isla—"

"You, Finn. I need you."

A groan cracks out of my throat, and suddenly, I'm gathering her up in my arms, holding her close to me as I bury my face in her neck. "I need you too," I whisper against her neck.

"Tell me who hurt me," she demands.

"My father did." And the truth is a stone weight removed from my shoulders.

"And who saved me?"

I can still feel the jab of the knife and my warm blood dripping down my arm onto her wound.

"I did."

"Tell me who my mate is." Her arms are tight around my neck, and I revel in the way she clutches me.

"I am."

There's electricity in the air, raising goose bumps on my arms.

"Will you kiss me now?" She loosens her hold enough that our gazes clash.

"I don't think I can stop with a kiss."

The woman I love told me I'm hers. My whole body is hot with need to show her that she'll never have a reason to regret her choice. That I don't need a drop of magic in my body to be the best mate a selkie has ever had.

"Then, don't stop." Isla leans in, flicking her tongue against my bottom lip.

Next thing I know, my ass is on the ground, and my woman is straddling me. Our mouths are so close that we share a breath, just before I tilt my chin up and claim a taste of my selkie mate.

11

ISLA

F INN KISSES me like he'll never get the chance to again.

Easing in and then taking, never breaking away.

I can hold my breath underwater for hours, yet somehow, this man gets me to start panting.

But a sudden realization has me pressing him away.

"No," he growls, dark eyes tracking my mouth.

"That was a convincing animalistic noise. I'm impressed."

"Isla." His voice comes out with a deeper rasp the second time as his fingers dig into my waist.

"I needed my mouth free to talk to you about something important."

When my pause stretches, he snaps forward, trying to capture me in another kiss. But I'm faster and a touch stronger than he is, holding him at bay.

"Eyes up, human. Focus on my face."

Finn's hungry gaze flits to my eyes and stays there, his dilated pupils showing just how aroused he is. Of course, I'm also sitting on a very prominent erection, so I'm not surprised.

"I'm focused," he claims. "*Extremely* focused."

"Good. I fell in love with you senior year, when you picked me first for your kickball team in gym class."

For a full count of five, my human just stares at me. "But that was after you thought Owen was your mate."

"I know. Which I told the gods was extremely inconvenient and cruel and that they should take the emotion away."

"Did they?"

"I thought so." Suddenly, I realize that I have permission to touch Finn, so I reach up and comb my fingers through his unruly mop of black hair. "Then, right before graduation, you ran back to my car to get my flip-flops after one of my heels broke. And I fell in love with you all over again."

With each word I speak, a smile creeps wider over Finn's face. "You've been in love with me since graduation?"

"Of course not!" I scoff. "I reminded the gods that they'd chosen Owen as my fated mate, so they *really* needed to get rid of the love I felt for you. And I'm positive they did."

"Is that so?" From the lowering of Finn's eyelids, I can tell he doesn't believe me.

"Yes. But then it was raining. That time at the coffee shop three years ago. And you came inside, all wet, with your shirt clinging to your chest." Now, I hook my fingers under his black T-shirt and tug the material off over his head to see the offending chest.

"You fell in love with me because I was wet?" His chuckle brushes against my neck as he leans in to press kisses to the sensitive area.

"That's ridiculous." I tilt my head to give him better access. "I fell in love with you again when you said you wished Folk Haven had a bookstore."

Finn straightens. "And that made you love me because ..."

I still remember him stepping up to me in line, his eyes

wide and searching as he said hello. Finn asked how long I was in town for, and I told him I was heading out again that afternoon. In fact, I had to leave right after getting my coffee if I wanted time to go to the bookstore in Atlanta before catching my flight.

And he said, with so much regret that it infused every inch of his body, that he wished Folk Haven had a bookstore.

"Because I think we were envisioning the same thing. The two of us getting coffee and then walking over to the imaginary bookstore, talking as we went, rediscovering each other. Then maybe making out between the shelves. And the fact that you wanted exactly what I wanted did it for me."

"Did you ask the gods to take the feeling away again?"

"Yes."

"Did they?"

"I pretended they had."

"Until when?"

"Until I saw your delicious butt sticking through that inner tube."

Finn barks out a laugh as his arms tighten around me. But I don't let him close off too much space, my hands intent on sliding down his torso until I reach his fly. He stills under the caress.

"If it's not clear, I'm trying to tell you that I love you." I undo the button on his shorts and slowly pull down the zipper. "I have for years even if I tried to ignore the feelings." I slip my hands into his pants and find the flap of his briefs. "And I never plan on asking the gods for it to go away again." I free his dick, the hard length standing warm and straight in my grip. "Because I need to love you."

Finn's forehead falls forward to rest against mine, heavy breaths bellowing as I stroke him.

"I love you too. Think I have from the day I met you."

Shifting forward on my knees, I position Finn's cockhead right at my entrance. In preparation for something like this outcome, I decided to come over here in a dress without any panties. No point in overdressing for the occasion.

"Finn."

At the sound of his name, he lifts his gaze to mine.

"I take my birth control pill promptly at eleven a.m. every day and have done so for the past three years. And it is widely speculated among our kind that mythics cannot contract venereal disease. Also, my gynecologist gave me a clean bill of health two months ago. What's your status?"

"I—oh hell—you mean, you want to ..." He's some kind of flustered, hands fisting in my skirt, eyes tracing over my face and then fixating on our laps.

"Finn. Status. Now. Or I'm climbing off you to find a condom."

"No STDs!" the man practically shouts. "I'm good. So good. Sit down. *Please.*"

I do appreciate being asked nicely. With a measure of control, I lower myself, focusing on the press, the push, the widening of myself to fit around the hard length of my human. When I've gone so far that my thighs rest on his, I realize a sheen of sweat covers my chest. My heart races. I feel everything.

"You're inside me," I tell Finn, untangling his hand from my dress so I can draw his palm up and press it flat against my chest. Directly over my heart.

"Hell, Isla. I never want to leave." He stares at our hands on my body the same way he used to stare at me from across the room. Like there's only one thing in the world he can see.

All he sees is me.

All I need is him.

Searching for more—the pinnacle I promised myself I'd reach to claim my mate—I begin to rock my hips. Slow at first, but then he groans, and the power of that sound infuses me, driving me on faster, harder, with unending love and absolutely no mercy.

"I wanted to take my time with you," he gasps out before both his teeth and eyes snap shut.

"I plan to take my whole life with you," I inform him while guiding his hand under the fabric pooling around my waist.

Realizing what I want, Finn takes over, his strong fingers finding and stroking my clit as I clench down on him with my inner muscles.

Curses and praises spill from his mouth, but his touch doesn't let up, and soon, I'm curling into him, my body shivering with a release even better than the ones he helped me with last night. Because this time, the word *love* floats in the air around us.

"Isla," he moans my name, his voice torn with it.

I plan to hear myself referred to in this manner many more times over the course of my life.

We have years to make up for, the ones when I naively believed I knew the will of the gods.

My mate and I sit, curled around each other, bodies heaving with gulping breaths that soon turn into giddy laughs.

"Your knees are going to give us away." Finn points out as he glances down to where I brace them in the dead leaves, no doubt smashing dirt into my skin even now.

"My skirt is long enough to hide them. But you'll have to hide your butt. Your shorts are a mess. I rode you hard."

He skips a breath at that and then smashes his mouth into mine, plundering a deep kiss I'm happy to have stolen.

Eventually, we convince each other that this is not the last, but instead a continuation of many intimate times together. Only then do we rise off the ground, doing our best to wipe away debris before walking hand in hand back to the house.

Where we discover an interesting scene.

"I need one that is mostly gray with just a small bit of blue in the corner," my mother announces.

"Here. Try this one." Mr. Hammond passes a puzzle piece across the table, where a partly finished picture of the Hoover Dam is spread.

"Mimosas are ready!" Finn's grandmother strolls in from the kitchen, a pitcher in her hands.

"Fantastic." My father stands from his chair, accepting a glass from her and holding it steady as she pours. "I've never had a morning cocktail, come to think of it. But I do like orange juice. And champagne." He takes a deep sip and then catches sight of us. "Isla and Finn are back. Did you two have a productive talk?"

Words remain just out of my reach as I attempt to understand the sight before me, where my parents are easily mingling with humans. This is what I wanted, but I half-expected to return and find they'd retreated to my car and locked the doors to maintain a safe barrier.

"We did." Finn raises my hand to his mouth to press a kiss to my knuckles.

"Oh good. It seems I was right." My mother nods to herself, attention still on the Hoover Dam.

That truly throws me off-balance. "What do you mean by *you were right*? It's not as if you knew I'd been in love with Finn for years. I barely ever admitted it to myself." In fact, I'm perturbed at her tone after tying myself in knots about how to convey this to them.

"You drew a heart around his picture in your yearbook. All four years." My mother could not sound less surprised with this situation as she examines pieces of the puzzle.

"You did?" Finn gives me a smirky grin I will likely have to kiss off his face.

"That's not proof of anything. I also circled Owen's picture."

"Only in the last two yearbooks," my father offers after another sip of his drink. "And you drew a square around him. In black marker."

"We thought you might be intending to harm him in some way. A blacklist maybe," Mama adds.

I find myself extremely miffed with this turn of events. "I did that because I thought Owen and I were meant to be together," I growl, knowing this is not a battle I have any reason to be fighting. "And because our *families* are similar," I say carefully, aware that Finn's grandparents are still in the dark about the magical creatures that live in Folk Haven.

Both my parents glance at me then, matching scowls on their faces.

"You and Owen MacNamara? Oh no. That would never do," my mother chides.

"He's too wild. Only follows the rules he likes. No. We prefer Finn." My dad raises his glass to my human, who seems to be fighting off a terrible coughing fit.

But then I see the grin grow wider and realize Finn is struggling not to laugh.

"Since when?" I press, unable to move past my parents' sudden acceptance of humans.

My father hums a happy note as he sips more of the drink. A noise he usually saves for only the most perfectly brewed cup of tea.

Mama takes up the explanation. "A few years ago, some men came to fish on the lake. They used *nets*." She grits out the word as if it were a curse, and to my family, it is. "The police were called, and they were escorted from town." Her fingers shake as she sorts through puzzle pieces. "But they left the nets in the water."

Anger rises in a slow tide through my body. *How dare they!*

"Finn dived for an entire week, searching every last one

out." My mother grants her attention to the human at my side, fixing her eyes on him. "We never properly thanked you for that."

"They were dangerous," my mate mutters, his fingers fisting in the back of my dress.

Both my parents nod, almost in unison.

Mama takes that moment to remember there's a pair of not-in-the-know humans in the room. She offers Finn's grandparents a tight smile. "I used to swim every day when I was a young woman. In the ocean near my home. When I was pregnant with Isla, I would still swim. One evening, I was caught up in a discarded fishing net. I almost drowned."

Mrs. Hammond gasps, and her husband wraps a comforting arm around her shoulders.

My mother nods. "I might have died if Patrick had not cut me free."

"You are a good man," my father says to Finn. "A protector of the lake and everyone living here. We would be happy to have you as part of our family."

The proclamation shoves through me, as if The Finned One speaks in my father's voice.

"Fine!" I announce loudly to the room, breaking the emotionally heavy moment I'm not sure how to handle. "You approve of the man I love. Fantastic. I will just shred all my well-planned arguments I had for convincing you that we're perfect together."

"You had written arguments?" Finn asks as he relaxes his grip to slip an arm around my waist.

His easy touching elicits only positive responses from my body, as if my skin recognized him merely as an extension of myself.

"Not yet. I was drafting them in my head. I planned to type them up tonight after this went badly. But now, everything is going perfectly smoothly, and I didn't plan for that. What do I do now?"

Finn cups my cheek with his hand, guiding my eyes to his. "Start typing up plans for our future."

EPILOGUE

ISLA

"D*id you get enough to eat*?" My love's voice pulls my attention away from the window.

My mind takes a moment to focus on the words he said. "Yes. Plenty. The water is distracting me."

Finn sets the plate full of foodstuff down and adjust the bag on his shoulder before wrapping me in his arms. Any other night, his embrace would be all I needed. But it's been a month since I wore my second skin, and my body longs to sink into my other form.

"Of course," he murmurs, pressing a kiss to my neck. "Let's walk down. Looks like Moira and Calder are already on their way."

He's right. I spy the two siblings stepping off the back porch of the MacNamara house, making a straight shot for the lake.

"You coming?" Owen sidles up to the two of us, his arms clutching his selkie pelt.

He grins easily, like he always does, but I get the sense he's more relaxed now that the truth is out about the night of my accident. The man actually apologized to *me*, not realizing I'd interpreted the event as a fated mates' catalyst. Turned out, Owen had known about Finn's crush, and he'd figured if I was interested in the human, I'd want to reveal my true nature on my own terms.

Because Owen is a good man who cares deeply, I found it easy to forgive the misunderstanding.

"So, you're sticking with the whole *dick out for the world to see*, huh?" Finn deadpans at his best friend, indicating Owen's naked form.

"You're mated into a clan of selkies. Better get used to some nudity." Owen claps Finn on the shoulder before strolling into the dark night, the pale globes of his ass cheeks the only moon on display.

Finn hooks an arm around my waist. "Are you wearing that robe for me?" he asks.

I glance down at the thick terry-cloth covering. "Yes." He frowns, so I explain further, "You have to spend the rest of the night without me. I thought you would appreciate my attempt to desexualize myself, so you don't suffer too much lustful longing while I'm gone."

"Lustful longing?" Finn snorts. Then, he shows how right I was when he pulls me to a spot on the back deck in shadow and presses me against the side of the house. "Okay. You're right. I'll miss you." Then, he fuses our mouths together, kissing me with enough heat that I almost forget the call of Lake Galen.

Almost.

He breaks off, panting. "That's not helping."

I pat his cheek. "We'll get better over the years. Besides, you'll like how I am tomorrow morning."

In the darkness, I make out the bright flash of his grin.

Selkies always get light-headed, almost drunk, after taking on our finned forms for the first time after a long stretch. When

I return to my human shape tomorrow, I'll be overly enthusiastic and handsy, which Finn said he can't wait to experience.

"Come on then. Let's get you wet."

I let him take my hand and guide me toward the shore. Soon, I overtake him, pulling ahead. When the water brushes my toes, a needy shiver rocks my body.

"Here. You give me the robe, and I'll hand you your skin."

Glancing behind me, I watch Finn carefully remove a shimmering mass from a bag slung over his shoulder. I shuck off my robe, so we can exchange. Though my selkie pelt begs to wrap around my limbs, I hold off long enough to steal another kiss.

"I love you." Wet clay slides along my soles as I step farther into the water.

"Be safe. I love you too." Finn remains rooted to the shore, waiting for me to finish the change and slide beneath the surface.

My human skin is suddenly sensitive, overexposed. I wrap my selkie skin around me, sighing in pleasure with the way the hide melds to my body. My limbs flex into their new shapes, and I allow the water to claim me.

Everything is right again, the inside of my body calming from a clamor built up over days. My mind eases, and I let the current take me.

For a time, I drift, blowing bubbles of acknowledgment to others of my kind who swim by. Some selkies experience a rush of energy, taking on this form, and they spear through the water, coaxing others to play and celebrate the freedom. I tend to drift toward meditative. Which might be why I seem to be the only one who notices when one of ours swims with purpose toward the mouth of the cove.

There is no law stating we must stay in this branch of Lake Galen during our change. But it is understood this is the safest place for us. I experienced firsthand what can happen when we stray. When I gave in to a desire to explore all those years ago, I ended up in the wrong part of the lake just as Mr. Hammond was speeding by. Lucky that Finn dived in and Owen followed me.

That acceptance of both their important roles in saving my life has me making a decision now. I won't let this member of my clan travel into the lake alone.

I follow.

The figure ahead of me doesn't meander. They have a destination. I flick my tail harder to keep up while spreading my awareness darting all around me. Finn was right that knowing about the perpetrator and how he's off the lake have helped ease some of my worries. But I still get the occasional nightmare.

The selkie disappears up ahead, and I realize they rose to the surface. Following suit, I carefully peek only my eyes above the water.

We're at a dock, one in a section of the lake not home to any selkie families. As the mythic removes his skin, I realize I've been following Calder, the youngest of the MacNamaras. He hauls himself onto the floating platform, approaching a woman. The dark-haired beauty from the party.

A human? Maybe a potential mate he wishes to pursue?

She must be someone special if he would reveal himself in such a way to her.

They embrace, and their actions slide into passionate territory. Just as I've accepted Calder is safe enough that I can head back, the woman tilts her head toward the lake. Purple irises glow bright in the dark night.

Not human.

Not selkie.

Another mythic of some kind.

I sink below the water and carefully retrace my path. Calder is not in any danger. Not at the moment anyway.

When it comes to selecting a mate, mythics pair either with

one of their own kind or a human. The first is easiest. The second is harder because they need to be introduced to our world, but it's still widely done with our kind.

But a partnership between two different mythical creatures carries a stigma in our community.

Silently, I wish Calder luck with his pursuit of love. He'll need it.

Because when mythics mix, that's how the world gets monsters.

The End

Thank you so much for reading A SELKIE'S SECRET. I hope you enjoyed Isla and Finn's love story! Do you want to spend more time in the mythic-filled Folk Haven? Check out the following books for more small town, sexy, fated mates romances.

SEDUCED BY A SELKIE

Delta Novac hates Folk Haven, and as soon as she's done cleaning out her father's mess of a house, she's giving the town her taillights. But after she dives into the lake to save a drowning man that's not actually in danger, she finds herself with a sweet and sexy selkie shadow ready to do anything to get her to stay.

SUCKER FOR A SIREN

Seamus MacNamara refuses to believe in the selkie mating myth: that his one true partner will rescue him from great danger. So, when the adorably beautiful barista he has a secret crush on gives him the Heimlich, Seamus ends up insulting her instead offering heartfelt thanks. Now he just wants a chance to redeem himself…and he's willing to go down on his knees to earn her forgiveness.

SWEARING AT A SEA MONSTER

Moira MacNamara takes shit from no one, and that includes Levi Abadi, the enticing, infuriating monster who thinks he can dictate what she does with her own property. She makes a deal with him, sealed in blood. But now she can't help noticing how her veins thrum with heat every time he comes near…

STAY IN FOLK HAVEN

You don't have to leave Folk Haven just yet! Keep reading for a sneak peek of *Seduced by a Selkie*, book one in the Folk Haven series...

SEDUCED BY A SELKIE

DELTA

When my father died, he left me a lake house, and I hate him for it. As if losing him suddenly wasn't bad enough, now, I'm back in this middle-of-nowhere town in northern Georgia, forced to set his estate to rights.

Estate. Ha. That word makes his house sound impressive. Maybe from the outside. But step in the door, and everything turns into a death trap.

When I got the call from Folk Haven's police chief about my father's passing a few months back, I half-expected the cause of death to be something more gruesome than a heart attack. Not that I wanted my father to suffer. They told me his death was quick, and even if someone had been nearby, there would have been an infinitesimal chance he could have survived.

With Dimitri Novac's hermit lifestyle, that chance had turned into zero.

Which leaves me here, sitting alone on the end of his dock in the early morning, listening to the hollow lap of the water against wood, contemplating Lake Galen and mortality.

Maybe my morbid thoughts manifest a response because,

suddenly, I'm sure I'm staring straight at a lifeless body floating facedown in the water.

"Oh hell," I mutter, scrambling to my feet, unsteady on the floating dock.

The higher vantage point shows me the same image. Just past the mouth of the inlet, maybe a hundred feet away, a person is rocking in the waves like the leavings of a shipwreck.

Adrenaline and panic make my decision for me. I rip off my long-sleeved shirt and unzip my jeans, pushing the denim off my legs without the hindrance of shoes because I walked down here, barefoot. Pulling on my muscle memory from a long-ago summer swim team, I dive into the water and plow toward the prone figure, using a strong freestyle. The distance first appeared closer than it is, and as I continue to pump my arms, I try to remember how long a human can go without oxygen and still survive.

Is it long enough for me to reach them, drag them to shore, and start performing CPR?

Doesn't matter. I have to try.

When I lift my head, shaking water from my eyes, I spot the lifeless form only a few strokes away. With a powerful kick of my feet, I cross the final distance. Despite my hope, the logical part of my brain informs me I am about to grab hold of a dead body.

Which is why I scream when the head pops up at my touch.

The man—because I see now that it is a man—jerks back at my holler, raising his hands above the water, as if surrendering.

"It's okay. I won't hurt you," he assures me in a rumble of a voice.

"You're not dead!" I shout, as if him being alive were an inconvenience.

His eyebrows creep up. "Would you prefer I was?"

"No." I suck in a deep breath, winded from my sprinting swim. "I ..." Words slip away from me as I glance behind him.

At this new angle in the water, I spy a pontoon boat floating outside the mouth of the inlet.

Unnecessary adrenaline keeps my heart pounding hard and makes it difficult to organize all this new information.

"Hey." The deep voice recaptures my attention, and I meet the set of soft brown eyes in an otherwise blockish white face. "Hi." He greets me again, his smile easing the harder angles of his jaw. "You were swimming up to a dead body?"

"I wasn't *sure* you were dead," I correct.

That only has him smiling wider. "You're here to save me?"

As understanding of the new situation dawns, I struggle to keep afloat—literally and figuratively. My body tries to remind me it's been a few years since I trod water for any length of time.

"Do you need saving?" My breathlessness comes from a combination of the swimming and his focused gaze.

At some point, we must have drifted closer, pushed around by the subtle lake waves.

The swimmer's hand rises from the water, catching a strand of my hair on the ascent. The black threads spill like ink about my pale shoulders, my skin turning a ghostly shade from the chill of the lake. He stares at where the lock wraps around his finger in a tentacle-like grasp.

"People rarely admit to needing help." His gaze laughs as his grin goes lopsided. "Please, continue saving me. Likely as not, I need it."

If I had time, I'd put in the needed mental energy to identify the subtext of his words. But a movement over his shoulder distracts me.

The good news: I don't need to come up with a response to his oddly philosophical statement.

The bad news: our conversation pauses because I'm transfixed by the sight of a head breaching the lake surface behind my not-dead acquaintance.

The appearance is only the beginning. One to my left. One on the right. All around me, more heads appear, all equipped with goggles and breathing pieces, identifying this crew as a gathering of scuba divers. Seems I've shown up in the middle of a scuba lesson. Soon, we're floating in a crowd of heads.

And every single one is facing me.

That's when I remember my outfit. Without my shirt and pants, I'm left with the most basic coverings. A matching bra and underwear set I got on sale at a department store. Both scraps of fabric are blue and covered in pictures of cartoon bananas.

No doubt, that's why they were on sale.

This group got an unobstructed view of my bargain boy shorts as they surfaced.

I hate this fucking lake.

I keep my curses to myself. "Well, looks like you've got this under control."

The man lets my hair return to the water as I paddle backward. Once I'm clear of the group, I turn on my stomach and swim back to my father's dock, possibly moving faster than when I thought someone's life was at risk.

Embarrassment is powerful fuel.

When I reach the dock, I grab the metal ladder and place my feet on the slick, algae-covered steps sinking below the surface.

"Please don't let them be watching me," I mutter as I pull myself out of the lake, soaked underwear clinging to my backside and rigid nipples. *Note to self: swimming in April is cold, even in Georgia.*

When I'm standing tall—because I refuse to cower and hunch over in my half-naked state—a quick glance behind me shows my audience is still watching the show.

"Fucking peachy," I mutter.

Thoroughly done with this miserable morning, I offer the

lot of them a salute, gather up my armful of clothes, and march toward the shore, reminding myself with each step that I will probably never see any of those people again, especially when I leave Folk Haven and Lake Galen for good.

So, what does it matter if they all have a permanent memory of soggy bananas decorating my ass?

Keep reading Seduced by a Selkie!

ALSO BY LAUREN CONNOLLY

Paranormal

Folk Haven

A Selkie's Secret (Book 0.5)

Seduced by a Selkie (Book 1)

Sucker for a Siren (Book 2)

Swearing at a Sea Monster (Book 3)—Coming January 2022

Casual Magic

Fire Magic & Ice Cream (Book 1)—Coming spring 2022

Seasonal Magic

Remembering a Witch (Book 1)

Wanting a Witch (Book 2)

Contemporary

Forget the Past

Rescue Me (Book 1)

Read Me (Book 2)

Resist Me (Book 3)—Coming soon

Standalone Novel

You Only Need One

ABOUT THE AUTHOR

Lauren Connolly is a Colorado Book Awards Finalist and an author of contemporary and paranormal romance stories. She's lived among mountains, next to lakes, and in imaginary worlds. Lauren can never seem to stay in one place for too long, but trust that wherever she's residing there is a dog who thinks he's a troll, twin cats hiding in the couch, and bookshelves bursting with the diverse stories written by the authors she loves.